This book, as always, I couldn't have completed without my wife Laura's murderous mind.

This is for Rachel, Wee Iain, Sarah, Lucy, Oisin, Saoirse, Amelia & Lucas

Chapter 1

Ellie was in a blissful state of comfort, that stage of sleep where you find the perfect comfortable spot in bed. She was aware of Bruiser snoring at the bottom of the bed and Bella letting out the occasional sleep growl. Kate was wrapped in her arms, her breathing shallow and calm. Bliss was the only word Ellie could think of as she snuggled in closer, inhaling the hint of coconut from Kate's shampoo.

A loud bang shattered Ellie's dream-world state. She heard doors in the house banging and then a voice bellowed from the hall.

"Right, you two get up! It's a busy day, lots to do!" Aggie shouted to them. Kate groaned her displeasure and buried her head under the duvet. Bruiser ran off to greet Aggie with a happy waggy tail.

"Get up!" the voice was louder now, Ellie cracked one eye

open to see Aggie standing in the doorway with her clipboard and a stressed expression on her face.

"And there's no use looking at me like that Katherine Mitchell! You were the one that decided you needed to get married in three months! Honestly, I don't know how I've managed all of this." she muttered.

Since they set a date, Aggie had been the epitome of a Bridezilla but in Mother-of-the-bride mode. In the past month she had reduced a florist to tears and a caterer to quit their business and go to find themselves in Tibet. The wedding organiser at Oran Mor, the old, renovated church where the ceremony would take place, had developed a nervous twitch anytime he was near Aggie. Peggy was still suggesting that they drug Aggie until the day of the nuptials and Ellie wasn't entirely sure if she was joking, but with five days to go, she was warming to the idea.

Ellie stumbled out into the hall bleary eyed to be handed a coffee by a sympathetic looking Peggy.

"She woke me up at 5am to ask about bridesmaids' underwear, why do I need to be interested in knickers at the crack of dawn?" grumbled Peggy. Ellie snorted a laugh and Peggy frowned at her.

"Sorry…underwear…crack of dawn…" Ellie explained.

"Oh god you're getting worse, it's Gavin's bad influence." Peggy said shaking her head.

"Thanks for the coffee, you're a life saver."

"No problem young'un, I've got one for Katie too. Where is she by the way?" Peggy asked as she looked back towards the bedroom. Ellie and Peggy peeked round the door and watched as Aggie was attempting to drag her daughter out of bed by the ankles as Kate held on to the headboard.

"Mum! get off me! I'm awake! Unless the house is burning down this is a bit excessive!"

"Katherine Mitchell get out of that bed this instant! We've got too much to do today!" Aggie was still trying to lift Kate from the bed but slipped and fell backwards on to the floor. Kate took the opportunity to scramble back under the duvet. It was when Aggie went in after her that Ellie and Peggy decided to leave them to it.

They sat in the kitchen drinking their coffee with matching exhausted faces. Ellie had been working late nights to try to finish paperwork before the wedding and Peggy had been away for her work recently, she had returned with a new medal in a box so it must have been a success.

The war between Kate and Aggie appeared to have ended as Kate limped grumpily into the kitchen and slumped into a chair beside Ellie. Peggy pushed her coffee over to her and Kate grunted in thanks.

"Good thing you're a writer with your oratory skills in the morning" joked Peggy. Kate was exhausted too as she had been working flat out to get her book finished. The stress and long hours had brought on an M.S. flare up, her leg was weaker than usual, and she was needing to walk with a stick for now. Aggie marched into the kitchen with her clipboard, her hair was tangled and sticking up as if she had been wrestling an animal, she glared at her daughter briefly before she addressed the group.

"Well now that we are all FINALLY..." another glare at Kate "awake, I'll run through what we need to do today. Ellie your dad and aunt Ann are arriving at the airport in two hours, young Gavin will be here soon to go with you to help with the luggage. Kate, you have a meeting this morning with your publisher?"

"Yes, so I don't see why I have to be up so bloody early when it's not for at least an hour yet!"

"Then we are picking up Seb and Rachel from the train station, I think they will be on the 1.15pm arrival from London. Have I forgotten anything?" she asked.

"No but while it's in my head, can you have a word with that sister-in-law of yours?" asked Peggy with a scowl.

"What's Val done now?" groaned Aggie in despair. Val was Kate's dad's sister, when her dad left when she was young, Val remained as the only member left of that side of the family.

"She phoned me last night at 11 o'clock to ask for Ellie's phone number." Ellie spluttered coffee everywhere.

"Me? What does she want with me?" she asked as she wiped coffee off her chin.

"She wants you round her house to do something about the gang of youths hanging around the area." Peggy said as she rolled her eyes. Val was a battle-axe that Peggy had many run-ins with over the years.

"Does she know that Ellie isn't a beat officer and doesn't actually do that?" Kate asked, incensed at her aunt Val's audacity.

"When would that stop the auld cow trying to get what she wants?" muttered Peggy. "The woman needs a slap more than anyone else I know".

"Margaret!" Aggie scolded her sister, although stopped short of actually defending Val.

"We should get a move on; Gavin will be here soon and you two aren't even dressed yet. Come on! Shift yourselves!" Aggie ordered them out of the kitchen.

Chapter 2

Glasgow Airport was busy at that time of the morning. Ellie had found a parking space that she knew would cost her a small fortune and she and Gavin walked towards the arrivals area.

"What time is their flight?" asked Gavin as he stood with his hands in his pockets and yawning.

"They should be coming through baggage collection by now. Why are you so tired?" she asked to the back of Gavin's throat as he had yet another jaw-breaking yawn.

"Ach Mhairi had me up half the night, she's got heartburn and her feet are killing her." he explained.

"Poor Mhairi, don't you have a scan to go to today?" Ellie remembered suddenly.

"Aye but not until this afternoon, they just want to keep an eye on the twins as we get closer to the due date."

"Will you stay conscious this time?" Ellie asked innocently.

"Ha ha very funny, I'd like to see your reaction to that news!" he grumbled.

The day Gavin found out that he and his wife were in fact having twins, he collapsed in the doctor's office. Ellie has never let him live it down.

"Gav if I was told I was having twins I would need sectioned!"

"What was with the atmosphere round at yours this morning by the way?" he asked in confusion. "Aggie and Kate looked like they were ready to kill each other."

"Do you remember what it was like to try to get Kate awake to catch an early train?" Ellie asked with amusement, she knew fine well that Gavin would never forget having shoes launched at him when he tried to wake the redhead at 6am to meet Ellie off a nightshift at Central Station for a weekend break.

"I remember…she really isn't a morning person, is she?" he shuddered at the memory.

"No, not when she's tired, which she is right now, and Aggie is marching round like a little general. They are so alike so it's actually funny to watch the two battle. So that's what you walked into this morning, Aggie bodily dragged Kate out of bed, and she was not happy about it." Ellie said with a chuckle.

"Rather her than me, it wasn't so bad when she was chucking trainers but when she hurled your Doc Martin boot at me, that hurt" he grumbled.

"Aww poor baby." cooed Ellie as she ruffled his head.

"Get off" he said as he slapped at her hand. They were so

busy play fighting that they missed the arrival of Bill and Ann.

“It’s good to see that Police Scotland’s finest are here to meet us, always alert and on the ball.” Bill said jokingly as Ellie and Gavin stopped fighting and stood up straight, slightly red in the face. Bill grinned at them and gave his daughter an almighty bear hug then shook hands with Gavin as Ann hugged her niece.

“I’ve given up hope of waiting for the day that you stop fighting boys” Ann quipped but her eyes were twinkling as she released her niece from a long hug.

“Hey! You were the one that taught me that headlock” Ellie joked back.

“That was you?!” Gavin replied shocked. “Aye thanks for that, she uses that on me when we fight about who gets the coffee!” Gavin whined.

Gavin muttered as he picked up Ann’s suitcase and they all headed towards the exit.

“How was your flight?” Ellie asked as she fell into step with Ann.

“Huh, a nightmare!” grumbled Bill. “Do you have any idea what it took to get her on that plane?! I was shoving calms into her like they were smarties, had her meditation stuff playing from when we left security and she spent 20 minutes in duty free looking for holy water to pour on the plane!”

“What? Ann we aren’t even catholic” Ellie said in confusion.

“See!” Bill said triumphantly. “See what a state she was in? Fair enough she only started looking for the holy water after I poured three large gin and cokes down her but still...nightmare altogether. All of this for a 25-minute flight."

"William Robert McVey you know perfectly well that I hate flying! I prefer getting the ferry over." she grumbled.

"No, you don't, you were hanging over the rail throwing up your dinner into the Irish sea the last time." Bill countered.

"Weren't you the ones slagging us off not five minutes ago about fighting like weans?" Ellie asked as her dad and aunt continued their argument all the way out to the car park.

As they all bundled into the car, Kate phoned. Ellie used hands free to answer the call as she backed out of her parking space.

"Hi honey, I'm just in the car with dad, Ann and Gavin, what's up?"

"Oh, hi everyone." Kate called cheerfully. All parties in the car responded with hellos. "Are you heading back to ours?"

"Yeah, should be about twenty minutes or so. Why?"

"Auntie Val called again" groaned Kate.

"What does she want this time?" asked Ellie as she caught her dad's eye as he mouthed 'who's auntie Val?'

"She wants us to come round to her house, she says she's got something for me but honestly, I think it's a ruse to get you over to sort out these kids she's moaning about. We'll have to go though".

"Yeah, no probs honey, we'll go as soon as I'm back, although what she expects me to do about a bunch of kids is beyond me."

"Knowing her she will want you to organise a firing squad. I'll see you soon then honey, love you".

"Love you too, bye." They hung up and Bill asked again "Who's auntie Val?"

"Kate's dad's sister. I've never met her but the stories about her aren't great, she sounds like a right old cow. She called Peggy to get me to come round and sort out some kids making a nuisance of themselves in her street."

"Hmmph, as if you would do that!" said Ann angrily. "You've worked hard to get to where you are and she's clicking her fingers like you're a hired security guard?! Oh no, don't bloody think so!"

Ellie had a feeling that she would have to keep her Auntie Ann away from Val for the duration.

Chapter 3

They arrived home shortly after, Gavin said hasty goodbyes as he ran to his car to go pick up Mhairi for the scan.

"What's his hurry?" asked Bill as he lifted suitcases out of the boot.

"He's got a scan on the twins to go to." Ellie said as she helped her dad with the cases and opened the main door to the building.

"Poor bugger, I was run ragged just with you when you were a baby!" Bill joked as Ann snorted behind him.

"You were where you? How many times did you call me to come round because you couldn't get the nappy on her or that time you thought she was playing hide and seek but was actually half a mile away?"

"Wait...what?" Ellie asked as Bill nudged his sister.

"Oh, calm down, we found you quick enough. You were heading back to the play park that we had just been at."

"What age was I?"

"You were three, honestly that day took about six years off my life!" Ann responded, shoving her brother gently. They were greeted at the door by Aggie who hugged them both in turn.

"Hello, good to see you again Bill, and you must be Ann, come in, come in you must be tired from your flight." Aggie ushered them through as Ellie came in with the cases.

"Aggie it's a half hour flight, they've not just arrived from Dubai!" Ellie started but was silent immediately from the glare Ann gave her.

"Oh, I like that, you must teach me that look, I've never seen her shut up so quickly." joked Aggie as Ann grinned and gave her a wink.

"Come through to the kitchen, I've done you some sandwiches and sausage rolls and a pot of tea, I'm sorry but I'll be leaving soon to go pick up my son and his wife." Aggie explained, clearly nervous about leaving guests unattended even when it wasn't her house.

"Aggie don't worry about us, Peggy said she will be our chaperone today, she's taking us on the Central Station tunnels tour." Bill said, as excited as a schoolboy at the prospect of a day of trains.

"Don't worry Ann, I've organised refreshment for you too." said Peggy from the doorway. "So, we'll have a bite to eat here and then set off." she said as she sat down and helped herself to a plate of sausage rolls.

Kate arrived back with the dogs as the tea was being poured. She ran over to Bill and gave him a big hug; Bill patted her cheek affectionately.

“Hiya love, good to see you looking so well.” he said as he let her go.

“It’s good to see you again Bill, Ann, you made it!” she exclaimed as she hugged Ann just as enthusiastically. “I was worried about your phobia of flying, was it ok?”

“Aye love it was just fine.” said Ann, Bill snorted, and she kicked him under the table. “Thank you for asking though, I’m glad someone cares.” Ann said pointedly.

“Teacher’s pet.” mumbled Ellie and Kate winked at her “No, I just know who’s in charge that’s all.” and Ann smiled broadly at her. Kate had flown over to meet Ann before the wedding and they had bonded instantly, Ann was a vociferous reader and loved crime fiction more than anything. Kate brought her an advance copy of her book and they had been firm friends ever since. Ann was a smaller version of Ellie, with more grey hair at the temples, she had piercing blue eyes that could either cut you down with a look or dance with laughter and mischief. Kate knew that Ellie considered Ann as her mother in all but name as she brought her up along with Bill. Ellie never talked about her mother, a woman who left without a word when she was barely out of nappies. Kate didn’t even know the woman’s name.

“We better get a move on if we’ve to get to Val’s before she calls again” Ellie said as she popped the last bite of a sausage roll into her mouth.

“Aye we better get a move on too if we are to make our time slot for the tour.” said Peggy, raising from the table and collecting plates.

“I’ll put your cases through to your rooms dad.” Ellie said

as she left the kitchen and grabbed cases and started dragging them down the corridor to Apocalypse Mansion.

Chapter 4

Val lived in the north of the city in a small street designed for the elderly to live in, like a retirement village but smaller. Neat little bungalows stood off the pavements behind neat little gardens. It had been named North Park Mews to make it sound exclusive. As they approached Kate muttered "Oh god she's already out waiting". Ellie followed Kate's eyeline and saw a very thin woman wrapped in a large cardigan standing at her garden hedge talking to an older man.
Kate and Ellie got out of the car and walked up the garden path towards Val and her visitor.

"Ah Katherine, I'm glad you've come. This must be Ellie then?" Val said quietly, Ellie couldn't miss the way Val looked her up and down. She obviously didn't like what she saw though, her face carried the expression you get when you smell something awful. Ellie already disliked her.

"Eric, this is my niece Katherine and her...um...friend, Eleanor. This is my neighbour, Eric." Val was about to continue but Ellie couldn't resist, she stuck her hand out to Eric to shake his hand.

"Actually, Eric I'm Kate's fiancé, we're getting married this week". She put on a dazzling smile and then turned back to Val with the same polite smile "Oh I'm sorry, you were saying something, please continue."

Kate stifled a giggle and grabbed Ellie's hand protectively against the glare Val was giving her.

"Yes…as I was saying, Eric and I were just discussing our neighbour watch patrol scheduled for tonight…"

"Wait? What? Patrol?" Ellie spluttered as she looked at these elderly people in front of her. Surely, they can't mean what she thought they meant.

"I'm glad to see Police Scotland's standard of intelligence has not dropped." Val said acidly. "Yes, dear PA-TROL" Val said slowly as if she was talking to a toddler before carrying on as normal. "We have a number of residents that form a group each night to patrol our streets, the Police do nothing, so we feel it's our civic duty to protect our homes ourselves."

"Val I'm sorry but that is very dangerous! You could get hurt, all of you, I'm sorry but I can't allow this…" Ellie was cut off by Val and Eric both laughing.

"Allow? Oh, dear I'm afraid you can't stop us. We are perfectly safe; Eric here was a Sergeant Major in the Royal Scots Fusiliers." Val explained as if he was James Bond himself before continuing. "We also have a retired military police officer and an ex-navy warrant officer in our ranks of volunteers, so we are more than capable thank you very much" sniffed Val.

"Val, Ellie is only concerned for your safety…" Kate began in defence of Ellie, but she too was cut off.

"Nonsense, we are perfectly safe and besides, if the Police were all that concerned for our safety, they would be out here at night patrolling so that we didn't have to! That's the trouble with folk these days, the old standards are gone. Every night we have these thugs disturbing us and what do the Police do? Nothing! Not even one patrol car comes round to look. I don't know why we pay our taxes."

"Quite right Valerie" chimed Eric.

'Oh god now he's starting' Ellie inwardly groaned.

"Now see here, we are trained professionals young lady and we are more than capable of protecting ourselves against some little hoodlums on bikes. We have to protect our own little patch of home, it's our duty." He actually stood to attention at this point, his moustache twitching as he stared off into the distance like the hero from an old war movie. Val looked at him as if he was the most wonderful specimen of manhood on the planet. Ellie pinched herself through her trouser leg to make sure she was actually awake, and this piece of theatre was real. She looked at Kate and she just rolled her eyes and shook her head as if to say, 'uh huh…this is what they're like all the time'.

Kate cleared her throat to get these Octogenarians out of their duty and honour stupor. "Val, you called to say you wanted to see me, what is it? Only we have a lot to do today so…"

"Oh yes very well, you best come in then. Eric I'll talk to you later." Eric actually saluted her like she was a General as Val turned to go into the house.

The inside of Val's house was exactly like Ellie would have thought, fussy and cold. There was lace on every surface, little fragile looking tables dotted all over the place holding delicate plants or china ornaments. Ellie felt too big for the room, it was if the walls closed in on you. She held herself still and upright, worried that she would knock something over if she breathed. Val was still muttering about the 'hoodlums' as she fussed around the room punching cushions into shape and picking imaginary dust off an aspidistra. She looked out the window and tutted loudly.

"There! See these are the little criminals we are talking about! Look at them!" she clicked her fingers in Ellie's direction as Kate's eyebrow raised, a clear indication that her temper was bubbling to the surface. Ellie decided to keep the peace and walk towards the window, she spotted a group of young men on bikes at the end of the street. They weren't doing anything other than filming themselves doing daft stunts on their phones.

"That one is the ringleader…look at him…he's got prison written all over him" Val sniffed as she pointed towards the tallest of the group. He was wearing a bright orange hoody with a ganja leaf printed on the front. Ellie turned as Val actually clutched the pearls around her neck.

"Oh, dear lord, drugs now?!" she screeched. "Oh, I need to sit down, this is too much to be borne it really is!" Val said as she sat shakily on a high-backed chair and started to fan herself with a copy of the Daily Mail. Ellie looked over to Kate who was stifling another giggle, she knew they were both thinking about Kate's own personal stash of medical marijuana that she grew at the house…best not telling Val that Ellie thought. Val finally composed herself and got to what she asked them over for.

"Now Catherine, I know my brother hasn't exactly been present in the past..."

"Present? Val, he disappeared before I could talk!" Kate said incredulous.

"As I was saying" Val carried on as if Kate hadn't spoken "it's a tradition in our family to pass on certain heirlooms whenever someone gets married." Val glared at them both, clearly not happy at having to perform this familial duty. "So, as you seem to be...um...coupling with Eleanor..." she actually used air quotes at that point and Kate's blood boiled.

"Married Val...we are getting married and if you can't even say it without distaste then why are you even bothering to come?!"

Val looked affronted at the anger in Kate's voice, but her face took on a cold impassive countenance once more as she continued once more.

"Yes, yes all very modern, but no matter what, it's my duty to pass on what is rightfully yours, excuse me one moment." Val got up and went into another room as Kate looked ready to explode. As they heard Val rummaging in a drawer Ellie grabbed Kate's hand and squeezed it gently and whispered "it's ok honey, don't let her get to you. We will be out of here soon. Don't give her the satisfaction of rattling you."

Kate nodded and seemed to calm down after taking a few deep breaths, she smiled at Ellie in thanks but kept hold of her hand to keep her grounded. Kate didn't often spend much time with Val, she always was a cold woman. Kate used to visit her once a week when she was a child but one day Kate was running around and accidentally broke a cup that was on a table. Val was so angry that she slapped Kate…she was only seven. That appeared to be the last straw for Aggie as they never visited after that incident.

Val reappeared with a small box, she sniffed disapprovingly when she spotted their linked hands but wisely chose to ignore it as she sat down once more. She opened the box and Kate looked inside, she gasped as she saw the most beautiful sapphire necklace. It was delicate and elegant looking. Kate wasn't expecting something so beautiful…especially not from Val.

"This was my grandmother's necklace. She got it from her grandmother upon the time of her marriage, that side of the family came from good stock, had a country retreat in the borders. You, Katherine, are the last female in the line so by rights…this is now yours." Val handed it over without another word and got up to gaze out the window once more. Kate didn't know what to say, she looked at Ellie who shrugged at her.

"Val…thank you…it's beautiful…I…"

"Yes well…look after it, don't lose it child." Val snapped, back to her old self once more. "Ah there's Doreen and Bobby, I must have a word about tonight. If you will excuse me, as you said…you must be busy".

"Val…please don't go out tonight" begged Ellie, now worried about what would happen to them.

"Nonsense, I can't let Doreen down, she's got a dicky hip! I can't expect her to go alone! Besides she used to be Military Police in the 70s and Bobby was a Warrant Officer in the Royal Navy"

Val escaped the room briskly as Kate and Ellie quietly followed her out.

"Did you see Eric? Drug emblems now!" Val called as she marched down the path.

"I saw Valerie, this place is turning into Sodom & Gomorrah" Eric said piously.

"Yes, well I would expect nothing less from that boy, his mother does ironing from the house." Sniffed Val as if this was all the evidence of bad breeding that was needed.

Val did no more than wave at them as she hurried down the street to catch up with Doreen. Ellie watched as Doreen looked curiously at them, but Val was intent on leading her away from them, so Ellie got in the car without another word.

As soon as the car door closed, Kate growled in frustration. "Did you hear her carrying on? His mum takes in ironing so he's bad blood?! The level of entitlement and snobbery astounds me! Who do these people think they are?! Why are they so much above others?" Kate was in full rant now, her eyes flashing with anger. "She forgets her own family past, my gran, her mum, was a cleaner who went to clean the posh West end homes back in the 50s. She worked herself sick to bring enough money in and to raise seven kids. My great gran was in service too. Val and her husband bought that bungalow off the council in the 80s and since then she's acted like the Lady of the Manor. All that claptrap about our family being well to do. If they did then it was back hundreds of years ago and they quickly lost the lot and died penniless. I researched the family history myself a few years ago and could find nothing. She's such an old snob it infuriates me, she hates Peggy you know?" Kate continued.

“Well, I think the feeling is mutual” said Ellie as she remembered Peggy’s reaction to having Val calling her.

“It’s all because Peggy worked hard and got into a good school, then onto Glasgow Uni and then the civil service. Peggy has earned a lot of money over the years, but you would never know it, she’s modest and invested it wisely. Val has always resented Peggy’s life.

“Hang on…if your family lost the lot and your gran was a cleaner…where did the sapphire necklace come from?” Ellie asked in confusion. “Surely your gran would have sold that to provide for the family?”

“I’ve no idea…perhaps she didn’t want to part with the last family treasure…it is beautiful though.” Kate whispered as she looked at the necklace once more.

Chapter 5

Kate and Ellie walked through their front door to be greeted by delicious smells coming from the kitchen, Aggie had promised to do a big family dinner for everyone tonight and preparations were under way. They barely got three feet into the living room though before a large ginger blur bolted towards them and picked up Kate for a bear hug

"Hiya sis" Seb said as he put Kate back down. He was grinning happily at her as his wife Rachel came in and hugged Kate and then Ellie too. Apart from hair colour, Seb and Kate looked nothing alike. Seb was tall, his arms covered in tattoos, and he was sporting a fisherman's beard, but the same eyes twinkled under all that hair as he then hugged Ellie. Rachel was tall and willowy with her black hair tied back in a neat bun.

"It's so good to see you both, how's the bar going Seb?" Ellie asked as they walked through to the kitchen.

"It's great, in fact we've just bought another place."

"That's fantastic!" Kate said enthusiastically. Is it the same type of bar?"

"No, we're branching out into something a little different. We're making a safe space for the Trans community in our area. We remember how hard it was for Rachel when she was transitioning, how hard it was to find a place she could just be herself. This new venture will be that, but it will be a café bar, open all day and Rachel's going to be running it." Seb said proudly as he took his wife's hand.

"That's amazing, well done both of you!" Ellie said with feeling as she hugged them both in turn.

"Thanks, I'm a little anxious about it but I feel like it's the right time for a place like this. But enough about us, let's talk bridesmaid dresses!" Rachel said as she dragged Kate over to the table as Aggie was setting places for dinner. Seb walked over to the cooker and peeked under a covered bowl. "Mum have you made dumpling?!" he asked excitedly as he went to pick a bit off. He didn't get within an inch of the clootie dumpling before Aggie had thwacked his hand with a tea towel.

"Ow! Hey, I only wanted a wee bit!" he complained.

"That's for pudding and I'm not having you pawing at it before everyone is here!" Aggie warned as she went back to setting the table.

"What did Val want Katie?" Aggie asked as she bustled back to shoo her son away from the food.

"Oh yeah, she gave me this" Kate opened the box that she had in her coat pocket.

"Wow is that real?" asked Seb.

"Seems to be, she said it was her grans and passed down

through the family."

"Is this the well reported wealthy side of the family?" Aggie asked. "It's all I heard about when your dad was courting me. You'd have thought they grew up in Buckingham Palace instead of a room and kitchen the way Val went on about it. Still, it was nice of her to give you it." Aggie conceded.

"Oh, I don't think she wanted to, she looked pained to give it to me, but her family duty took over. I don't think she approves of my deviant lifestyle" quipped Kate rolling her eyes.

"Can't wait to meet her" mumbled Rachel.

"She won't say a word to you I promise, Val's ignored me since I was a teenager and I turned down a job working with Uncle Howard. He was a plasterer" Seb explained to Rachel and Ellie. "I think they wanted me to take over the business, you know after their son passed away...but I was never any good at it, so I said no...she never spoke to me after that." Seb said, a hint of sadness passed over his eyes, but it disappeared just as quickly when he heard raucous singing coming from outside.

"What's this now?" groaned Aggie. She didn't have to wait long to find out. The singing got louder and then in crashed Peggy and Ann, they were holding each other up and laughing away like school kids. Bill was bringing up the rear...well he was until he walked into the wall.

"The cultural train station tour was a roaring success then?!" asked Aggie over the din, giving her sister the stink eye.

"Shhhh Aggie, we are still having a cultural discussion" slurred Peggy as she tried to stop Ann from sliding down the wall. "In fact, you are just in time to hear us recite poetry. Ann you first, the stage is yours." Peggy swept her arm theatrically, the gesture lost most of its elegance however when she smacked Bill in the face at the end of it. Ann stood up, well she leaned on the wall for support as she composed herself, she cleared her throat and began.

"There once was a barmaid from Sale

Tattooed on her chest the price of ale

And on her behind

For the sake of the blind

Was the same information in Braille."

Ann took an unsteady bow and then introduced Peggy. Peggy stood tall and looked out to her captive audience.

"There once was a fella called Reg

Who went with a girl in a hedge

Then along came his wife

With a big carving knife

And cut off his meat and two veg"

The two of them collapsed on the floor in fits of laughter at their own hilarity. Bill decided that he should attempt some propriety, so he stood tall and attempted an apology.

"We are so sorry dear lady if we are a few moments late, we stopped off on the way for a little winter warmer..." The rest of what he was about to say was lost the moment he tripped over Bella and fell over the couch.

"Oh god dad, what are you playing at, you don't even drink!" groaned Ellie as she ran forward to pick Bill up.

"Aggie I'm so sorry, he doesn't drink so he's a complete two-can-dan." Aggie surprised them all by bursting out laughing.

"It's fine Ellie, it's usually me that ends up in this state with Peggy so I'm happy to see the other side of it for once." She was still laughing as she picked Ann up off the floor, who by now only had one eye open.

"Let's get this lot to their beds for a few hours, I'll keep dinner warming until they sober up a little."

They half carried half dragged the drunken trio to their bedrooms to sleep it off and then returned to the living room to chat for a while.

A little later Aggie sat upright and stared at Kate.

"Kate, let me see that necklace again." Kate handed it over and Aggie looked at it properly, her face paled a little.

"Mum what's wrong?"

"I remember this necklace, it belonged to Val's mother last time I saw it..."

"So? She said it's her grandmothers and that it was passed down, so her mum probably did have it for a while." Kate said reasonably.

"No Katie...the old woman was wearing it on the day we buried her! I was at the funeral; it was open casket, and the old girl was wearing it. Val must have nicked it off the old dear's body!"

Chapter 6

It was late when they finally got round to having dinner, but an enjoyable evening was had. Kate was already in bed when Ellie came through after making sure everyone was settled. Ellie sat down to take her shoes off and get undressed for bed, she was looking forward to a bit of a lie in after a long day. The Universe must have heard her plans however as her phone started ringing before she had even got to her socks.
"McVey" she answered with a sigh.

"Ma'am, I'm sorry for the late call, I'm PC Simpson, I work out of Maryhill station. I had a call to an assault and one of the witnesses has asked for you specifically...she um... she was very persistent about it Ma'am."

"Asking for me? What's the witness's name?" asked Ellie, although with a sinking feeling she already knew who would ask for her by name.

"She...um...she said to tell you it's auntie Val." PC Simpson said as she cleared her throat uncomfortably.

“OK, I apologise if she’s giving you any trouble PC Simpson, give me the details and I’ll be there soon.” Ellie found a pen and paper to jot down the location, although she needn’t have bothered, it was at the end of Val’s Street. Kate had been listening to this exchange with her features darkening as the minutes passed. As Ellie hung up, Kate got up and started finding clothes.

“Honey…what are you doing?” Ellie asked in confusion as she watched Kate angrily hopping on one leg trying to get jeans on but falling as her balance went.

“What am I doing? I’m coming with you! If you think I’m letting Val get away with summoning you in the dead of night like you’re her personal security guard, you’ve got another think coming!”

When they pulled up to the Mews, they noticed that everyone in the quiet area was out in the gardens watching the drama. There was an ambulance parked beside the marked Police unit. They spotted Val standing at the back of the ambulance with a young officer that must have been PC Simpson. They got out of the car and walked towards them, there was a biting winter wind that cut through clothes and made Ellie shiver slightly as she regretted not putting a larger coat on.

“Ah, finally you’ve arrived!” Val snapped and Ellie had to grab Kate’s arm to keep her from doing harm to Val in front of the Police.

“PC Simpson I am so sorry about this” Ellie said quietly. “What happened?”

“She wouldn’t say until you got here, she was adamant

about it, but we arrived and saw that an older gentleman was lying on the ground with a head injury…"

"Don't ask her Eleanor! Was she here? No." Val interrupted, and it took all of Ellie's patience to remain calm as she turned to Val and politely asked "Ok Val, what happened?"

"Those little hoodlums nearly killed Eric while we were on patrol!"

"Did you see that happen or are you assuming that was the case, Val?" Ellie asked knowing Val's prejudices.

"Well, who else could it have been at this time of night? We had split up to patrol the streets, Doreen and I took one way, Eric another and then Bobby took the back alley. I had stopped in on Mrs Willis on the way to make sure she was ok, she's housebound and feels safer if we check on her. When I came out of Mrs Willis' house, I heard Eric shout, so I ran towards his voice. I found him lying on the path, his head bleeding. Doreen had arrived a moment before me and then Bobby after. We picked Eric up, he said he had been hit from behind so didn't see who did it; but I know!" Val nodded her head importantly. "It's that Neilson boy, the one I showed you earlier."

"Val, you can't just accuse him if you didn't see the attack…" Ellie began but Val cut her off.

"Oh yes I can! Eric was attacked in the area that they hang about in; they were up there earlier this evening drinking and carrying on. Eleanor if you don't do something then we will go to his house and make a citizen's arrest!"

"Right enough Val. I'll go see him, just go home now all of you" Ellie addressed the crowd of pyjama wearing pensioners that had crowded around the ambulance.

“Simpson, do you know who she’s on about?” Ellie asked quietly.

“I do Ma’am, Kai Neilson. He lives with his mum up in the high flats. He’s a known trouble-maker.”

“Fine, you come with me as you know the lad. Kate what do you want to do?” Ellie turned to Kate.

“Pick me up at Val’s when you’re done…I want a word with you Val” Kate said in a quiet tone that Ellie knew well…Kate was furious. Ellie left before Kate started on Val properly.

Chapter 7

Ellie and PC Simpson arrived at Kai Neilson's front door. There were lights on in the living room so at least she wasn't disturbing them too much. The knocked on the door and a tiny woman answered it, she was probably about Ellie's age but looked older around the eyes…tired. The woman sighed as she looked at PC Simpson.

"What's he supposed to have sone now?" she groaned.

"Sorry to disturb you Denise, we've had a complaint about Kai. Can we talk to him?"

"Come on in Sara." Denise said quietly as she stood back to let them through, obviously Simpson was a frequent visitor Ellie thought as she passed into a small hallway that led to a neat living room. The only thing out of place was the piles of ironing sitting on the couch and the ironing board up in the middle of the floor.

"I'm sorry, I've got a large order from one of my regulars due to be picked up in the morning." Sara muttered as she lifted the clothes off the couch for them to sit. "I'll go get Kai; he's playing some game on his PlayStation." Denise left the room and PC Simpson looked after her sadly.

"She's a good woman, she tries her best with Kai but it's tough for her. She's got a daughter with severe disabilities that needs round the clock care. Her husband walked out years ago and Kai went off the rails...and then she missed a Universal Credit meeting because her daughter took a fever and she rushed her to hospital...they sanctioned her benefits, so she gets nothing. That's why she does the ironing, it's a way to make money but be here for her daughter."

"That's a hard life" Ellie whispered, in awe at this woman's strength as she understood now why Denise looked exhausted. Denise arrived back with Kai sloping in after her, his hands deep in his pockets as he scowled at them.

"What have I done now?" he growled as he slumped into a chair looking insolent and defensive.

"We've had a complaint Kai, where have you been this evening?" Ellie asked.

"I was out wi ma pals earlier just hanging about, making videos of tricks and that...then I was here. Why? Who's said what?"

"We've had a report of an assault on an elderly gentleman that occurred about an hour ago. Would you know anything about that?" Ellie asked.

"Nuh, that's nothing to do wi me, is it one of those auld coffin dodgers down there?" Kai pointed in the direction of Val's street. "They're always on at me and my pals, probably deserved a slap" he grumbled.

“Kai!” Sara snapped to shut him up and then she turned to Ellie “It can’t have been him, if it was an hour ago, he was here. He was helping me get Ruth ready for bed.” Denise explained.

“Mum it’s none of their business” Kai roared at her as he stood up. “She’s told you I was here so that’s the end of it!” and with that he stomped off and slammed his door.

“I’m sorry about that” Denise whispered, “his temper has got worse lately, ever since he was sentenced to the Young Offenders at Polmont, he’s been a changed boy.”

“What was he charged with?” asked Ellie.

“Possession of Class A with intent to supply” Denise said flatly. “He told me he was only doing it to get money for us, I begged him to stop…” Denise said tearfully.

“And has he?” Ellie asked gently.

“I don’t honestly know, I’ve not found him with anything so as far as I know, he’s stopped.”

“Thank you for your time, Denise, oh by the way, what time did Kai get in tonight?” asked Ellie.

“Just after 9pm, he knows I can’t lift Ruth on my own now that she’s getting bigger. He’s always in for 9 to help me with her, sometimes he goes back out but not tonight. He’s been playing games in his room ever since.”

As they left the flat, she closed the door quietly behind them and Ellie had never felt sorrier for a woman in all her life.

Chapter 8

Ellie arrived back at Val's and thanked PC Simpson but said she could go now. She walked into the house, and you could have cut the atmosphere with a knife. Kate was perched on the edge of the sofa glaring at Val as another woman that Ellie recognised as Doreen was handing round cups of tea. When Val spotted Ellie, she stood up.

"Well? Is the little criminal in handcuffs?" she asked, a self-satisfied smile on her thin lips.

"No, he's not Val, it wasn't him." Ellie said, suddenly exhausted as she sat beside Kate and squeezed her hand gently.

"Don't be stupid of course it was him! Little thug…I mean you only have to look at him to…"

"Val!" Ellie cut across her, goaded now. "It's not him, he has an alibi now I suggest you let the matter drop and let the local police handle the investigation into Eric's assault.

"An alibi my foot! I bet that mother of his has vouched for him, thieves the lot of them...I'll tell you this..." Val started but she was stopped by Doreen who put a hand on her arm.

"Val enough now. There's nothing more the police can do unless they can disprove his alibi. That's not likely as none of us saw what happened...drop it now." Doreen said quietly but firmly. Ellie nodded her thanks and remembered that Doreen was Military Police in her youth so perhaps she understood the difficulties more than the rest of them.

"Oh ok, but I'll be watching him. One foot out of line and I'll have him, you mark my words." She sat back down and angrily snatched up a garibaldi biscuit. Kate got up to leave, Ellie was thankful as she didn't want to stay here a moment longer.

"Val I've got final dress fittings for me and the bridesmaids tomorrow. Would you like to come?" Kate forced a smile to her lips.

"No hen, I'm going to be visiting Eric in hospital and then I've got the bingo."

Doreen walked to the front door with them, and she stopped Ellie just as they were leaving.

"I'm sorry that we wasted your time this evening, I didn't know that she had asked for you until you arrived. I would have talked sense into her had I known."

"Not a problem, just promise me you'll keep her from doing anything stupid? And please can you stop the night patrols, it's too dangerous and tonight proved that." Ellie said earnestly and Doreen nodded. They left to try to get some sleep, Kate still hadn't calmed down and all the way home she was cursing Val uttering a long malediction that culminated in her threatening to make a voodoo doll of her aunt.

Chapter 9

The next morning, Ellie left the house as early as she could politely do so. Kate, Aggie, Peggy, Ann, Rachel and Mhairi were all going for dress fittings and a bottle of bucks fizz had already been drained. Bill looked like a deer in the headlights around these merry and very loud women. Ellie took pity on him just before she left.

"Dad, would you mind taking the dogs on a nice long walk?" she said with a smile and the relief on Bill's face was a picture, he practically ran for the leads. They left the house together, Bella not thrilled at the prospect of a long walk in the frosty morning.

"Thanks love, I didn't know where to put myself in there. Seb disappeared to make phone calls once Aggie started talking about the stripper on her hen night." He went pale at the recollection of the story.

"No problem dad, once you're back, grab Seb and go for a long breakfast somewhere and then it will be time for your kilt fittings and that takes ages. You'll both be out of the house for a long time" Ellie said with a wink.

"you're a good lass, when are you getting your suit fitted?" he asked as he put his free arm around her shoulder and walked her to her car.

"Not until this afternoon, so I'm heading to the office to finish up some stuff. After today I'm on leave, on call though in case of emergency. Well...good luck dad, if you go down to the end of the road and turn right, you'll find a great wee place for breakfast." She kissed his cheek and got into the car, she watched as Bill wandered off towards the park with the dogs, a slight spring in his step now that he had an exit strategy in place.

When Ellie got to the office, she was pleased to see Gavin waiting at the door for her, coffee in hand.

"You're a lifesaver" she groaned as she took the cup from him. "Anything come in?" she asked as they walked towards her desk.

"Nothing new overnight that we know of, so hopefully just a bit of paperwork today and you're off. Are we still leaving to go for fittings after work?" Gavin asked as he tasted his coffee and winced, clearly there wasn't enough sugar in there, he got up to add more in the kitchen.

"Yeah, your lovely wife is already at ours with the rest of them getting ready for dress fittings. How did the scan go by the way?"

"All good, everyone healthy and as they should be. Mhairi's been looking forward to today...aaah, that's why you're here so early, you got yourself out of the mad house before they all got too wild." He chuckled. "You mean to tell me that you abandoned your poor old father to that lot?" he shook his head "some daughter you are" he joked.

"No, I gave him and Seb an escape route before I left, I'm not heartless. Aggie was regaling them with the stripper story" she said pointedly, and Gavin froze.

"The one from her hen do? The story she told last Christmas when she had one too many snowballs and then re-enacted on me?" he asked, reliving the memory and the PTSD of a worse for wear Aggie trying to gyrate on his lap. "I never felt so used." he said, horror in his eyes. Ellie went over and patted his shoulder.

"There there big guy, it's over now".

Ellie spent the rest of the morning responding to emails from the procurator fiscal, HR and several case updates requested by the Chief Constable. She was glad to get rid of all the paperwork that had mounted up recently. She was just finishing a last email when PC Kent gets a call, Ellie spots her looking furtively over at her and then responding on the phone "...well...um I'm not sure if the boss is on shift to deal with this...ok...hold on and I'll ask." Kent put the phone down and walked cautiously over to Ellie.

"What's happened now?" groaned Ellie.

"Sorry Ma'am, there's a PC on the phone from Maryhill, she says they've turned up a body with a head wound. She wanted you to know that the wound and attack looks identical to one you dealt with last night."

"Oh no...what's the name of the PC?" asked Ellie but she already knew.

"PC Simpson."

"Do we have any details of the victim?" Ellie was scared

that one of the 'patrol' had got themselves killed.

"Yes, Simpson has named the victim as Kai Neilson."

"Oh shit" she exclaimed as she got up from her chair and grabbed her coat. "Tell Simpson I'm on my way, text me the location of the body Kent" she called as she left, Gavin hot on her heels. As she ran all she could think was 'Please, please tell me that those old codgers haven't gone too far!'

Chapter 10

Ellie and Gavin pulled up behind PC Simpson's car and got out. Kai's body was found at the children's playpark that separated the estate and Val's street. As they walked towards the scene, they spotted Dr Brett kneeling in front of a body that was sitting slumped on the swings, blood stained the back of his hoody.

"Morning Doc, what have we got?" Ellie asked as she pulled gloves on. Dr Brett looked up curiously. "I thought you were off getting ready for your nuptials?"

"I was supposed to be, but this one is sort of something I was dealing with before."

"How have you been dealing with this? Is this part of a serial killing that I don't know about?"

"No..." Ellie sighed and made sure she wasn't in earshot of any of the local officers "Kate's auntie Val lives here and has been complaining about this boy, her and her cronies have been patrolling at night like some neighbourhood watch on HRT and last night one of them got attacked... hit on the back of the head."

"Aah...now I see, ok then I better let you know what I've got so far. This young man has been dead since approximately 1-2am according to his body temp and lividity. It was cold last night so I can't be more accurate. I won't know for sure until I get him back to do the post-mortem but if I was a betting woman, I would say cause of death was that wound on the back of his head. Heavy blunt object has done the damage, but I can't tell you any more just yet."

"Have forensics been over this area?" asked Gavin as he looked around.

"Yes, they were here before I was. There's prints everywhere but they're kids prints mostly. The ground this morning was frozen solid so no fresh footprints in mud or anything useful like that. The team are already sifting through debris and prints taken this morning."

Ellie stepped a little closer and looked at the wound, it looked almost identical in location to Eric's. This made her think again about the vigilante grans, they were hardly likely to attack one of their own. So, who else is around this area that fancies cracking old men and teenagers over the head? So far, the victimology didn't make sense to Ellie.

"Doc, I'm going to get my team to send over pictures of the injuries inflicted on an older man last night. Would you be able to compare the wounds to see if they were inflicted by the same thing?"

"I might be able to, I would at least be able to say if they are similar. Have them send it over and I'll look."

Ellie thanked her and walked back towards Gavin; he was looking around at the houses surrounding the park.

"Someone must have saw or heard something Els, there's houses all around here."

"I know, we need to canvass the neighbours, get statements and someone needs to notify his mother." Ellie said, suddenly aware of the heartbreak that they were about to inflict on that poor woman.

"Els, you have a fitting; we can cover this stuff. I'll get Kent and Harris down here to collect statements and check if there's any CCTV in the area and I'll notify the family, there's nothing more that can be done just now anyway."

Ellie knew he was right, she needed to trust her team, she nodded and then when she was about to say something he pointed in the direction of her car "Go woman, if you miss the fitting Aggie will bury both of us in shallow graves."

Chapter 11

Aggie, Peggy, and Ann were all sitting waiting for the dresses to be unveiled. Aggie seemed to be constantly on the verge of tears, she openly wept when she walked into the shop and saw a huge meringue style wedding dress and had to be steered away by Peggy mouthing apologies to the shop assistant as they sat down.

The bridesmaids came out first, Rachel and Mhairi were dressed in matching burgundy empire waist dresses and Aggie burst into tears again.

“Oh, girls you look beautiful!” she exclaimed as she dabbed her eyes on a tissue that Peggy seemed to have a never-ending supply of.

“Even though I feel as if I’ve got a beach ball stuffed under here” Mhairi joked as rubbed her bump.

“Mhairi this dress shows off your bump in beautiful way” Rachel said.

"Easy for you to say when you're all tall and elegant. I feel like a Les Dawson character."

"Mhairi shut up you look gorgeous, and you know it" shouted Kate from behind the curtain. Kate opened the curtain and walked through. Aggie wailed all the more and even Peggy had a lump in her throat when she saw her niece. Kate was wearing an ivory silk dress that flowed down to a small, elegant train. It had a Bardot neckline and delicate lace sleeves, Kate had designed the lace herself, it was little harps and thistles linked together, Northern Ireland and Scotland linked. When Ann heard this description, she also burst into tears.

"I really hope all these tears are a good thing" said Kate as she watched her family collectively weeping into shredded tissues. But they all nodded emphatically before blowing their noses.

"Will this go well with all of your outfits?" asked Kate as she looked towards the family.

"I think so dear, I got a lovely silver dress and chiffon coat from that shop in the West end" said Aggie, pleased with her purchase. "And Peggy got a lovely chiffon three-piece trouser suit in the same place in a lovely aquamarine colour."

"I got my outfit in Belfast before I came over, full length royal blue dress and cape coat to match. The woman in the shop said it brought out my eyes." Ann said with a smile.

"They all sound amazing...I'm glad that you're all here with me for this...it's not something that I ever thought would happen to me" she admitted as Rachel squeezed her hand.

"I thought that too for many years...but when your soul mate arrives...you just know right?" Rachel said and Kate nodded with a smile.

"Although to be fair, I think my brother is punching slightly" Kate joked. She turned towards the mirror to look at the dress once more, she hoped Ellie would like it.

Ellie walked out of the fitting room to see what her dad and Seb thought of her outfit. She stood before them in an Ivory coloured suit, the wool trousers hung low on her hips and were paired with an embroidered ivory waistcoat and a white silk shirt. She put her hands in her pockets and shuffled uncomfortably at the silence before her.

"I mean...if you don't like it..." she muttered, embarrassed as she thought maybe it didn't look as good as she had imagined but when she looked up, her dad was crying.

"Oh, love you look beautiful" Bill whispered as he hastily wiped his eyes with a hanky. "Your gran would have loved to have seen you now." He said proudly with a smile.

Seb walked round her, and wolf whistled. "I think my sister is punching" Ellie laughed and then assessed both men.

"Well, you both look very handsome I must say." she said. Both men were in Worsted black 'hidden tartan' kilts with matching waistcoat, jacket, and sporran. Their ties were burgundy to match the bridesmaid dresses. With Seb's hair colour and huge beard you could imagine him running around the highlands 1000 years ago.

Just at that moment Gavin ran in, breathing heavily. “Sorry I’m late” he wheezed as he bent over to catch his breath.

“How did it go?” Ellie asked as Gavin was ushered towards the fitting rooms by an impatient fitter.

“Wait missus, hold on for one minute” he muttered as he detangled himself from her clutches. “Kai’s mum lost it Els, she was wailing something awful. I’ve left Sarah from family liaison with her, and she’s called the social workers to see if they can get her some help with her daughter. As for the fogie brigade” he said with a scowl “They’re up in arms over the attack on Eric and want the police…i.e., you to do something about it. The Chief came down to see me before I left…he’s been getting calls from some of that lot and I think he wants them off his back…he um…” Gavin faltered, he didn’t want to give her this news. “He wants you to investigate the murder and the attack…before your wedding.”

“Is he kidding me?” she groaned in frustration. “I get married in three days, what does he expect me to do in that time?”

“I don’t know Els…he didn’t look happy about having to make the decision any more that I am in telling you. Off the record he said that one of those old folk had connections to the policing minister so reading between the lines I think political pressure to resolve this has been initiated on the Chief.”

“Wonderful…I mean it’s not like I’ve got anything to do this week.” She growled before she turned towards her dad to explain the situation. In the blink of an eye, Gavin had been snatched away by the now victorious fitter.

“Dad can you tell them all what’s going on? Promise them that I will be there for every appointment that I’m supposed to be at…but otherwise I’ll be at work.” She said sadly.

“I’ll tell them love, by the sounds of it you don’t have much choice in the matter. Do what you need to do, and we’ll try to keep you up to date with wedding stuff.”

Chapter 12

Ellie and Gavin are back at Val's street after Ellie was able to prize Gavin away from the fitter with promises that he's still the same size as he was last time. Harris and Kent are standing on the path not far from them, when Ellie gets to them, they both look sympathetic, it would appear they all know that she's been asked to investigate this.
"What have we got so far?" Ellie asked as she looked around, the neighbours were all out observing.

"Ma'am, we've canvassed the area, and no one saw or heard anything after the commotion raised during the first assault." Kent said as she read from her notebook. "No one heard any further disturbance after the ambulance and police left. There's three houses that had no answer though." As Kent read out the house numbers, Ellie noticed a man in his late 60s standing in his garden listening to every word. He was pretending to be busy, but Ellie doubted he usually polished the leaves of his plants, especially not in his slippers. As Ellie made eye contact with him, he bounced forward like an excited spaniel.

"If I may be of assistance again officers?" he began and Ellie heard Harris mutter "Oh god not him again" before saying in a louder voice "Yes Bobby, what can we do for you?"

Bobby stopped in front of Ellie and saluted. "Warrant Officer Robert Lewis at your service Ma'am" Ellie wasn't sure how to react to this so just smiled back at him.

"Mr Lewis, how can we help you?" she asked him.

"Well, I couldn't help but overhear that you have a few unanswered doors? I can help you there you see the numbers this young lady read out are the houses of Eric, Doreen and Val"

"Ah I see, is Eric still in hospital?" Ellie asked.

"No, he was discharged this morning but with some good painkillers, he's probably out for the count. As for Val and Doreen, they volunteer down at the community centre, they make the tea and sandwiches for the groups being held down there"

"Thanks Mr Lewis, we'll make our way down there to see them." Ellie turned away and started walking back to the car.

"Harris, have you had any joy finding Kai's friends? They might have a better idea of who had it in for him"

"No Ma'am we've not been able to so far, we're waiting for Kai's mum to settle down a bit and then we'll ask her for details. Until then we've got officers knocking on doors in Kai's block."

"OK, good work so far. Make this your priority today, I want those boys in for questioning. They might be in danger themselves and I don't want any more violence in this street. Speak to PC Simpson from Maryhill, she's likely to know Kai's friends as it appears she was a frequent visitor up to Kai's mum, we'll go down and interview Val and Doreen…trust me it's a job you don't want" Ellie muttered as she got into the car.

Chapter 13

The Community Centre was not far from Val's street, it was situated behind the block of flats that Kai and his family lived in. Ellie and Gavin walked through the main doors and were met with a dull rumble of noise, there was a toddler group playing in the main hall. Ellie watched as tired looking volunteers chased after nippers who were drawing on each other or trying to eat the glue, she turned to Gavin with an evil grin "That's going to be you soon, your nice pristine carpets covered in felt tip and Ribena."
"Don't start me on that, I'm already having a panic attack over my favourite fleecy bedding…nothing nice in my house is baby proof"

"Poor diddums." quipped Ellie as she scanned the room once more. "I'm not seeing them in there so let's check the other rooms."

Most of the rooms were empty, there was a small room in which the local benefits liaison officer was in session with someone, diligently pouring over bundles of paperwork in an attempt to explain the complex benefits system to the poor guy sitting opposite her. They moved on and soon found a group sat in a circle talking quietly, Ellie checked the sign on the door. This group was for the families of drug addicts. Ellie spotted Val walking briskly towards a long table in the back, she was setting up sandwiches.

“There’s the woman herself, let’s go have a chat, we’ll do it in that wee kitchen off to the side.” Ellie pointed towards a door beside the sandwich table. They walked through the room, taking care not to interrupt proceedings, although Ellie could feel them being watched all the way to the kitchen.

Val was filling a massive pot with hot water for tea and Doreen was perched on a stool, her walking crutch beside her, as she buttered bread for sandwiches. Val noticed them first and put the pot down.

“Well hello Eleanor, what brings you here? Have you heard about the petition we are drawing up to get these little hoodlums off the street?” she asked, her eyes narrowed in vindictive glory.

“No Val we’re here on official business, I’m not sure if you’ve heard but this morning, we found a body, beaten to death at the children’s’ playpark at the end of your street. The victim has been named as Kai Neilson, the so-called ‘ringleader’ that you are campaigning about.” Ellie said quietly as Doreen gasped.

“Oh, how awful, his poor mother” she whispered.

“Oh, Doreen don’t be so soft! One less piece of scum in the world as far as I’m concerned.” Val said indifferently as

Ellie wondered how on earth Kate could be related to this woman.

"We are taking statements from everyone in your area, as you two were both out when Eric was attacked, we were hoping you could tell us what happened once we left? Did you hear or see anything unusual?" asked Gavin, his eyes were hard on Val, clearly Gavin wasn't a fan either.

"Well after that horrendous experience we both went into Val's for a cup of tea" explained Doreen.

"Indeed, for the shock you know" added Val.

"What time were you there to Doreen?" asked Ellie.

"Well after the tea, we must have both fell asleep. I remember resting my eyes for a moment and then looking at the clock and it was after 2am! I woke Val so that she could go up to her bed and then I went home. It must have been an adrenaline crash after all the excitement from earlier." explained Doreen.

"That's what I remember too, I was chatting about the petition and then I must have dozed off as the next thing I remember is Doreen shaking my shoulder awake and telling me to get to bed or I'll suffer in the morning with my back. I didn't see or hear anything as far as I can remember." Val said.

'They had alibis at least' thought Ellie but no new information for her was a bit disappointing.

"Thank you, ladies, you've been very helpful" said Gavin as he got up to leave, Ellie followed.

"I hope you find whoever did this, I won't feel safe knowing there's someone out there attacking people." Doreen said as she worried with the sleeve of her cardigan.

“We’re going to try our best” Ellie said kindly as Val scoffed but Ellie didn’t rise to it.

They walked back through the room as the group seemed to be breaking for tea. Once they got outside Gavin almost exploded.

“God Els that woman! I mean no offense to Kate but what an old battle-axe! Is she coming to the wedding?” he asked, and Ellie nodded. “I better keep my aunt Janet away from her, I don’t want to have to apologise for her rag-dolling the aunt of the bride.” He said and Ellie could see he was serious.

“Don’t worry about it, she would have to join the queue at this point.” Ellie grumbled as they headed back to the car. She looked at her phone as a message came through. “Kent has found Kai’s friends, they’re at the station now.”

Chapter 14

Two boys were sitting in interviews rooms, both looking nervous. Ellie walked up to Kent as soon as she arrived.

"Good work Kent, where did you find them?" she asked.

"I didn't, PC Simpson called me, they were being arrested for possession and she knew we wanted a word with them. This one is Ryan Summerhill, age 19 and a record of theft and possession charges going back to when he was 12." Kent read from the file as she looked through the window at a tall and skinny looking youth, his face pock marked but his eyes fearful as he looked around.

"Any violence charges?" asked Ellie.

"Nothing in his record Ma'am" Kent confirmed.

"And who is contestant number 2?" asked Gavin as he peered into the room.

"That's Jamie Gambon, he's 17 with similar priors to Ryan and Kai as they always seem to be together when they're arrested. No violence in his record either" Kent pointed out. "It makes no difference though Ma'am, they can't be suspects." Kent explained. "At the time of the murder they were in Maryhill police station being questioned about the drugs found on them. That's how Simpson knew where they were. They couldn't have attacked Kai."

"Nothing's ever easy" muttered Ellie. "Well, they are still important witnesses to the events prior so I should have a word with them. We'll take Ryan; he looks the jumpiest." She decided. "You take Jamie, Kent".

Ellie and Gavin entered the room and sat at the table in front of Ryan, he looked at both of them nervously.

"I didnae kill Kai" he said in a panic. "Honest I didnae!"

"I believe you Ryan" Ellie said calmly. "But I want to talk to you about last night, you might be able to help us. Can you tell me about your movements from late evening onwards?"

"Aye...um...we were hanging about, just having a laugh and that...Kai went home for a while to see to his sister. We went to the chippy while we waited for him. Once we had our chips we walked up towards Kai's flat, we met Mick on the way but then we heard sirens and flashing lights, there were polis all around that old folk's street. We thought they had phoned the bizzies on us again, so we legged it. Me and Jamie ran towards his house as its closest, but Mick tore off the opposite direction down through the weans park towards the shops."

"Who's Mick?" asked Ellie.

"Michael Adams, he's our pal. He's on parole so didn't want lifted." Ryan explained.

"I see, then what happened?"

"We watched from Jamie's bedroom window and saw the ambulance over on the street, so we stopped panicking you know, they weren't there for us, so we went back out to meet with Kai."

"What time would this have been?" asked Ellie.

"I dunno…midnight maybe?"

"Did you meet up with Kai?" asked Gavin.

"Naw…we got halfway to his when we were stopped by some jobsworth polis who searched us and found a bit of blow. We got huckled and spent the night at Maryhill. My maw's gonnae kill me" he muttered.

"She will if you keep doing this son, it's no way of living." Gavin said gently, knowing all too well the tragedy that can befall you if you mess with drugs. His brother hadn't been dead for long and it still hurt him although he would never admit it.

"Oh aye? And how else am I supposed to bring money in? My maw works two jobs and is constantly skint…I hate that she has to work that hard. With my record I'm hardly likely to get a decent job, am I?" Ryan said sullenly.

They left the room just as Kent finished with Jamie. "What did he say?" asked Ellie.

"Only that they didn't see Kai, they went to the chippy and then to his house when they saw police everywhere. They stayed at his for a while then went back out and got lifted almost immediately. Oh, and there's another one of them…Mick? He's still unaccounted for." Kent said as she read from her notes.

"We got the same story, I believe the. Right Kent, I want you to make finding Michael Adams your top priority, if he's done a runner then we need to treat him as our prime suspect in both the attack on Eric and the murder. I need all the information you can find on Kai's life; does he have any enemies or rivalries that we should know about. Get Harris to go back in and interview tweedle dum and tweedled dee about that, they will know better than anyone. Call me with any updates, I've got to go home, there's a party planned." Ellie explained.

"I'll pick up Mhairi and will be there soon" smiled Gavin as they left the office.

Chapter 15

As Ellie and Kate had refused to have a hen do, Aggie had organised a family party instead. The family were all there as well as Gavin and Mhairi and it was going well, Aggie had decorated the living room with gold and silver balloons and had pushed all the furniture to the sides so that there was a dancing space. Seb and Rachel were slow dancing in the middle of the floor, happy in their own private world. Ann and Aggie were in the kitchen chatting and bustling back and forth with food, although Ellie noticed that they kept sneaking new bottles of red wine back to the kitchen with them. Kate and Mhairi were flipping through the music to look for a song which they found. Whigfield's Saturday night started blaring out of the speakers, interrupting Seb's slow dance momentarily, but he just continued swaying along with the upbeat music. Kate helped Mhairi off the couch as they both stood and started to do the dance in perfect synchronisation.

"Are you two mental?" exclaimed Gavin. "Neither of you

should be dancing!" he was fretting.

"Ach Gavin lighten up; a wee bit of dancing isn't going to harm the kiddies. If Kate falls over, at least she's on carpet" Mhairi shrugged, and Kate agreed as she carried on with the hand movements.

Ellie was smiling at their antics as she watched from her perch on the window. She delighted in seeing Kate so carefree and watched her adoringly as she stumbled her way through the jumping parts of the routine. She had almost forgotten that Val was there, she had invited herself when Kate mentioned it the night before. She had obviously had a few drinks by now, she was staggering a little bit, spilling sherry as she went. She kept looking around the room and sniffing. She started passing comment about the décor but with the music blaring, only the people closest to her could hear her. "Don't think much about those curtains…Kate's worth a few quid I'm sure she could afford better than this" she continued as she actually ran her fingers along the fireplace to inspect for dust. "I mean…that's why Eleanor has been sniffing round her isn't it? To get her hands on Kate's money…out for what she can get that one" she carried on in an acid tone. She was interrupted by Peggy gruffly taking her by the arm "I think you've had enough Val, Seb's going to take you home now. Right Seb?" Peggy said loudly as she chucked car keys at Seb's head.

"Oh…err…yeah, come on Val, I'll take you home." He quickly kissed Rachel and helped Peggy take Val to the car.

Ellie was perturbed, never had she thought that people would think she was a gold digger. Kate's wealth had never really been an issue for them, Ellie made good money at her job, more than enough for her needs. Is that what people thought though? She was brooding over Val's words when Rachel gently touched her arm.

"Don't listen to her Ellie, no one thinks that. She's just a spiteful old woman that's obsessed with money. She came out with similar comments about us when we got together...amongst other things" Rachel said quietly but then she perked up. "Don't let her ruin your night, look Kate is having a ball...focus on love not hate" she said wisely, and Ellie knew she was right. Peggy came back through the door, her face flushed with anger.

"I'm so sorry Ellie, she doesn't speak for any of us, I hope you know that." Peggy said quietly, making sure that Aggie, Ann, and Kate didn't hear. "That woman is a complete and utter b..." she was interrupted by a knock at the door. Ellie was closest so she went to answer it. She was confused to see a tall young police officer standing at it. She didn't recognise him, and she had no calls to say anyone was coming. Only then did she notice that he was carrying mini speakers and that he had a slight whiff of baby oil. She groaned as he pressed play on his music and sauntered into the middle of the room in a seductive manner.

"Oh, my Christ!" Aggie screamed, mortified. "I think I might have hired him when I was a bit squiffy" she confessed as the man started gyrating. "I thought seeing as you weren't having a hen do that it would be funny to hire a strippcr."

"A *Male* stripper mum?! Really?" exclaimed Kate as he attempted to gyrate in her direction. She shot panicked eyes at Ellie, but she was too busy laughing to be of much use. Mhairi had no qualms as she dug about in her purse for a fiver and slipped it into his pants, this earned her a lap dance that she enjoyed immensely…and Gavin didn't. Aggie rushed over to the stripper before Gavin killed him and tried to apologise.

"I'm so sorry young man there seems to have been a dreadful mistake" she said as she tried to stop him, Mhairi was having none of this and grabbed hold of him to keep him on her lap. Aggie switched the music off and finally got the man away from Mhairi's clutches.

"As I was saying young man, we're terribly sorry….is that you Lewis Conroy?!" she yelped. The man looked mortified and started gathering up his clothes in a hurry.

"It is you Lewis, remember us? We used to live in the same street, I used to watch you for your mum…how's she doing these days? Her feet still giving her bother?" Aggies asked as Lewis went crimson and wished he was anywhere in the world but here in this moment. "Yes Mrs Mitchell…I…I remember you…. yes, my mum is well thanks…I better go" he took off at a sprint, tripping over his trousers as he attempted to put them back on.

"Another party success" quipped Ellie who was in stitches at the scene that was playing out before her. All thoughts of Val long forgotten. She was wiping tears of laughter from her face as her phone rang.

"Kent, what have you got for me?" Ellie asked, still chuckling slightly.

"Ma'am…I'm sorry to interrupt your evening…but you said to call if anything happened." Kent sounded unsure that she was right to call, Ellie was having a good time and she hated to interrupt.

"It's fine Kent, what have you got for me?"

“We’ve found Michael Adams”

“Oh good, have you talked to him yet?” asked Ellie and there was a pause on the line.

“No Ma’am…we found his body.”

Chapter 16

Ellie and Gavin were stood in the rain in the alleyway behind Val's local chemist. A tent had been erected around the body and Doctor Brett was examining him.

"Who found the body Kent?" asked Ellie as she looked around, the alleyway was shared by the row of shops in this area, large bins lined the walls.

"The chemist found him when she was locking up, she was taking the rubbish out to the bins on her way out and spotted his feet, she called us immediately." Kent explained.

"What's her name? We'll need to get a statement from her."

"Her name is Melanie Stokes; uniform have taken her home to get a statement from her there…she's in shock" explained Kent as they watched the Doc come out of the tent and motioned towards Ellie

“What have you got Doc?” asked Ellie as she and Gavin entered the tent. She saw a young man lying face down, blood staining his hair and face. He was quite large, Ellie guessed at around 20 stone.

“Death occurred due to being hit with a blunt object in the back of the head…exactly the same injury that Kai sustained.” Doctor Brett said as she sighed and looked at Ellie. “He’s been here a while Ellie; I would say his time of death was within hours of your other victim.”

“Why did no one notice him lying here?” asked Gavin in confusion. “These bins are communal, that takeaway must have bene out here to get rid of food so why didn’t they see him? They would have seen him immediately from their back door?”

“I wondered that too” Kent said as she poked her head through the tent. “So, I did a bit of googling and found that this takeaway was shut down last month by environmental health…rats apparently”.

“Doc any clue what they’ve been hit by yet?” Ellie asked.

“Something thin and cylindrical is all I can say Ellie, there are no splinters or other particles in the wounds on Kai, so I don’t think it was wooden. No defensive wounds on this victim so he was surprised by the attack. I’ll know more when I get him back to do the post-mortem, but the attacks are very similar.”

“Was he dragged in here to hide him, or do you think he was attacked here?” asked Ellie.

“I think he was attacked here; I can find no drag marks on his shoes; it will be impossible to check for blood though with all of this rain.”

"If he was dragged in here then we would be looking at a murderer with a lot of strength...look at the size of him, Gavin could you drag him in here?" asked Ellie, thinking aloud.

"Just about, if I was motivated and scared." said Gavin.

"Nah...he must have been killed here...he's too big to have moved quickly without being spotted. The killer must have hoped that the bins would have hidden him here for a while. The chemist will have been closed by then so no one would have been around here until the next day." Ellie decided.

"Doc, let me know what you find, as soon as you can eh?" Ellie begged and the Doc nodded.

"I'll be as quick as I can Ellie, anything I can do to help speed things up I will."

"Kent, get Michaels' background information ready for the morning and get Harris over to his next of kin to notify them before it hits the news. If they find out there's potentially a spree killer in the area, we will get no peace." Ellie said as a feeling of dread settled over her. She had a bad feeling about these attacks.

Chapter 17

The next morning Ellie was hunched over the kitchen table clutching a cup of coffee as if it were a lifeboat on the Titanic. She was exhausted, she felt like she was running about trying to please everyone but not achieving anything. There was an alarm bell going off in her head that she couldn't shake, that the person responsible for the attacks is far from done and Ellie was no closer to finding them.

Bill walked in to see his daughter brooding over her coffee, he knew she was drowning in her thoughts, she had been brooding like this since she was little. He poured himself a coffee and sat down beside her.

"That was some party last night eh love? Good craic so it was." He sipped his coffee as Ellie nodded absently at him. "Ellie, tell me about your case…what's getting to you love?" he gently prodded.

"I've got two victims dead with similar head injuries,

they're young, small-time dealers by the looks of it. My team is looking for any potential rivals out there that might want them out of the way..." she went silent again.

"But something doesn't fit?" he guesses.

"Yeah...Eric, Val's neighbour was attacked in the same way on the same night the first victim died. If it was drug rivalry, why hit an old man out walking on his own? The victimology isn't making sense to me and it's putting me off my game I think" she chuckled a little at the realisation.

Bill sat quietly for a moment, sipping his coffee deep in thought much like his daughter then he turned to her "Do you want to know what I would have done?" he asked quietly. She nodded, her dad was a good officer back in the day and she trusted his judgement. "If you're getting stuck on the victimology, maybe it's because you've only got three to work with, so any discrepancies turn into large issues...why don't you check the local area for similar attacks, say in the past year. It could be that there are more victims out there that have been marked down as gang or drug related deaths and not investigated properly. If this ends up being the case, you will at least have more data to work with to compile a decent profile."

"That's not a bad idea...why didn't I think of that" she muttered as she grabbed her phone and dialled Kent. "Morning Kent, I need you to run something for me, can you do a citywide search for similar attacks in the past 12 months? Yeah...anything that looks like a single blow to the back of the head. Can you get that together for me by the time I get in? Great you're a star, tell the team I'll bring the coffees in with me." She hung up looking a little brighter and she smiled at Bill "Thanks Dad" she said softly.

"I didn't tell you anything you didn't already know love, but you've got that much going on in that noggin of yours that you just needed a different perspective is all." He said squeezing her hand as they went back to sipping their coffee. Their peace was interrupted by Aggie bustling through with her clipboard and Rachel walking briskly behind her.

"Now you need to go pick up the flowers dear while I get the room decorations, we don't have much time to get organised and I'm afraid it's just the two of us this morning as Katie has meetings..." she carried on listing the multiple jobs needing done that day as Rachel nodded and kept silent, she had learned not to interrupt Aggie in mid-wedding plan. Kate had shuffled in behind them looking exhausted, she yawned so deep her jaw cracked as she slumped beside Bill who took pity on her and poured her some coffee.

"Ah girls, do you have the wedding music to give me? I'll need to give it over to the celebrant on the day" Aggie said over her shoulder as she continued listing tasks with Rachel. Ellie glanced at Kate who looked as confused as she did. Kate mouthed 'wedding music?' and Ellie shrugged. Bill took pity on them and whispered out of the corner of his mouth "You need to choose the music you will be walking down the aisle to, and some others tracks as background"

Kate looked panicked; they didn't have time for this today so Ellie answered Aggie in the calmest voice she could muster. "We have them picked Aggie, but our memory stick cracked when we were about to download them from the laptop. I'm heading out today to get a new one so we will have it for you later". This seemed to mollify Aggie and she bustled away again; they heard her shouting for Seb from the hall.

"Thank god I'm out all day" groaned Kate and Ellie agreed, they wouldn't have to deal with Aggie until the rehearsal that evening.

Chapter 18

Ellie had arranged a team meeting for first thing in the morning, she brought them all coffee as promised and then stood at the front of the room and looked at them all. "Who's first?" she asked. Gavin stood up with a file in his hand.

"We've got the final post-mortem reports from Doc Brett, Kai and Michael were hit with the same item. The same wound type was present on both skulls and no other marks were found defensive or offensive. She also was very excited by finding a blond hair stuck to Michael's wound that wasn't his. She just this morning confirmed that it was Kai's hair. Doc's theory is that the murderer caught some of Kai's hair when they attacked him, then it was transferred from the murder weapon onto Michael." Gavin finished as Ellie looked thoughtful.

"If we ever get this guy then it will be great evidence if we can get trace on that murder weapon. Excellent, anything else found?" she asked.

"Both boys had money and drugs on them, both hidden in their socks so drugs are very likely the link here" Gavin went on. "Also, it's been confirmed that they died where they were found, blood splatters were found on the swing set and on the bins." By this point Kent was bobbing in her seat like a school kid.

"Kent did you get anything from the search I asked you to carry out?" Ellie knew she had; her eyes were dancing.

"Yes Ma'am, the search has brought up three more young men within a local 5-mile radius that have died from a single blow to the head, all of them were suspected drug dealers and all were killed in the past 6 months." Kent finished, pleased with this news.

"Excellent work Kent, I want you to get the autopsy and forensic files for each of those cases. Send them over to Doctor Brett, explain the urgency to her and let me know what she thinks of them. If these cases can be linked, then I think it's safe to assume that we have a serial killer on our hands and that the targets are drug dealers within the North and Northwest of the city. Harris, get each victim's criminal record, I want to see if there are any links between them there too. Brilliant work everyone, thank you" Ellie said with feeling, at last they were getting further forward in the case.

"Ma'am!" bellowed Harris from his desk, he had his phone in his hand. "Trouble down at you soon to be aunt-in-laws street."

"Oh, what now?" she moaned.

"The vigilante grans have caught hold of Ryan Summerhill and Jamie Gambon; they've tied them up and are threatening them." Harris relayed to her still holding the phone to his ear.

"Oh, for Christ's sake! What have I told that lot about interfering? I'm tempted to arrest every one of them for obstruction!" she growled as she grabbed her coat. "C'mon, I'm going to need the lot of you for this one, if I go alone, I might strangle them!" she called over her shoulder as everyone scrambled up after her.

Chapter 19

Ellie and the team arrive once more at Val's street to find quite literally a baying mob. All of the neighbours were crowded around Eric's house jeering and shouting, most of them wearing their slippers and a few of the ladies were out with curlers still in their hair.

"Jesus, would you look at this?" muttered Gavin as Ellie gave up trying to get through the crowd by car and just ditched it where she stopped. "Everyone be on the look-out for torches and pitchforks." Gavin quipped as he got out of the car. They pushed forwards through the throng of people and finally got to the front. Bobby, Val, and Eric were standing, pleased with themselves, by Eric's garden fence. They had handcuffed the boys to the fence, both were pale and looking terrified of the oldest baying mob Ellie had ever seen. Ellie had seen enough.

"WHAT THE HELL IS GOING ON HERE?!" she roared over the crowd, and they stopped jeering immediately. Eric bounced forward, full of importance and with a smug smile on his face.

"What's happening here is that we are doing the Police's job for them!" he had raised his voice a bit so that the hard of hearing in the crowd could hear him properly.

"Eric what you've done is kidnapping!" Ellie said in exasperation. "Where did you even get handcuffs from?"

"They're Doreen's from her Military Police days, handy things, and it's not kidnapping, we made a citizen's arrest!" Eric huffed importantly although some of his bluster was ebbing away at the thought that he could be in trouble.

"Eric there is no law that allows a citizen's arrest in Scotland, a member of the public may use MINIMUM force if there is a serious crime being committed. That does not mean you can chain teenagers to fences!"

"They were selling drugs! Ina caught them giving drugs to her granddaughter. She's only fifteen! Ina, Bring your Sophie over!" Val shouted through the crowd. A tall woman with an enormous nose rushed forward dragging a girl by the arm, the teenager looked mortified at her gran's actions but stood in her school uniform staring at the ground.

"Sophie, tell the officers what happened." barked Ina. Sophie rolled her eyes but under the harsh glare of Ina and Val she relented.

"I bought a wee bit of weed off Jamie, it was just a wee bit for a party tonight" she grumbled.

"Did you hear that? They're corrupting our children with this muck!" shouted Val and the crowd woke up a bit and started jeering again.

"ENOUGH!" roared Ellie once more, goaded beyond endurance now. "ALL OF YOU GET BACK TO YOUR HOMES... NOW!" she barked at the crowd as she nodded to Kent and Harris who took the hint and started to herd the mob away. Ellie turned back to the main players in this drama. "Sophie you will need to make a statement, get your grandmother to bring you down to the station either this afternoon or tomorrow morning." Ellie looked at Ina and she nodded her assent to the plan. Ellie then headed towards the still chained up boys. "Have you got anything on you that I should know about?" she asked them quietly. The boys looked at their shoes but didn't answer her. "I thought so...DI Bickerton can you search Jamie while I search Ryan?" Ellie asked, her eyes trained on Ryan...he looked scared now. Both boys were then searched, nothing was found in their pockets and Ellie could see a bit of confidence working its way back to their expressions and decided to wipe that away as soon as possible. "DI Bickerton; search his socks and shoes" she said, Ryan now looked stricken. As shoes were pulled off, several things fell out. "What do we have here?" ask Gavin as he used a gloved hand to pick up a roll of bank notes and several small bags containing various drugs. Ellie and Gavin turned to both boys in unison and started to read them their rights. Bobby handed Ellie the cuff keys, she unlocked them and then secured Ryan with her own cuffs as she led them back to the car. Gavin and Harris took stewardship of the detainees while Ellie walked back towards the three people still standing in the street.

"Right, you lot, you got lucky this time that those boys had stuff on them. If we hadn't found that then you were getting arrested for false imprisonment Eric. You've been attacked once already this week, I don't want a repeat of that incident, please stay in your homes at night...no more patrols. There's someone dangerous out there and I don't want any further casualties...am I clear?" they nodded at her, and she sighed "Val remember rehearsal is tonight."

"I'll be there" Val said quietly, through constrained anger that no public execution was going to happen today.

Chapter 20

Kate got home from her meetings to find that everyone was out, including the dogs, Bill and Ann must have gone for a walk. Kate sighed as she walked through the corridors towards the basement mansion area. She was exhausted and sore; her leg had been painfully going into spasms all morning. She had decided on a quick swim in the pool to see if that would help stretch her muscles out a bit to stop the pain.

The pool was designed by Peggy to help her niece keep her strength and was built into the absolutely huge panic room basement extension that Peggy had gifted them and was now nicknamed 'Apocalypse Mansion'. Kate got into her swimming costume and eased herself down into the warm water to slowly do laps of the pool. She knew there was a fine line between the exercise helping her muscles and the fatigue kicking in that could land her in bed, so she swam only for enough time for her to feel her leg muscles stop being so tight that they were painful. She slowly walked out of the shallow ramp end of the pool, designed to make it easier for her to enter and exit without climbing a ladder, she made her way around the side of the pool but when she got to within ten feet of the pool loungers she collapsed.

“Ouch! oh you’ve got to be fucking kidding me?!” she growled into the heavens. Her right leg had lost all power and buckled underneath her, she couldn’t get up and there was no one around to help. Anger and frustration almost overwhelmed her as she used her upper body strength to half lift and half crawl her way over to a lounger where her phone was sitting. She used her good leg to lift herself onto the lounger and she sat for a moment to regain her strength. Anger was coursing through her, she hated the unexpected aspect of her illness, the way it just hits with no warning. She knew from experience that her leg would regain its strength soon, it was just a matter of being patient.

Kate must have fallen asleep as she opened her eyes when she heard Ellie shouting her name from the main house, her swimming costume was completely dry. She looked at her phone, she had been lying there for an hour. She heard Ellie’s footsteps coming down the corridor and she sat up, attempting to look like she had just been chilling down here for a while, she didn’t want Ellie to worry, she had enough stress to be getting on with.

“Hey honcy, what are you doing down here?” Ellie asked as she planted a kiss on Kate’s lips and sat in the lounger beside her.

“What am I doing?...by the pool?...in a swimming costume?...waiting for the number 7 bus.” Kate quipped, forced her tone to be light even as a pain shot through her leg and up her neck.

"Ha ha oh Queen of sarcasm. I meant why? You don't usually swim on busy days unless you're sore." Ellie asked, concern on her face as she looked down and spotted bruises on Kate's leg. Kate looked down and cursed quietly, she had been hoping Ellie wouldn't notice.

"Honey what's wrong? Are you ok?" Ellie asked as she gently took Kate's hand in her own. Kate just sighed.

"I'm ok sweetie I promise, my leg is just being problematic today. I thought a swim would ease the muscles and it did...what I didn't bank on was the bloody leg giving way on me when I was walking out so I went down like a sack of tatties."

"How's it feeling now?" Ellie asked as she started to massage Kate's tense calf muscle.

"Still sore but I can feel it easing a little. I'm a bit scared sweetie...what if this happens when I'm walking down the aisle? It's not going to look great for the bride to go arse over tit, in a nice frock, is it?"

"Oh, honey don't worry about the wedding day, Seb's walking you down so he will keep you close and make sure you're sure-footed if you're worried about it." Ellie then paused to bring up something that would help but Kate would fight against. "Have you thought about using your stick on the wedding day? Just to keep you steady if you need it?"

"I'd rather not have to if I can help it, don't want a stick ruining the wedding photos." She murmured.

"Are you worried about that? Why? Get a posh one, you could rock that the same way Selma Blair does, make it an elegant edition to your wedding couture" Ellie said with a grin and she was relieved when she noticed Kate's mood lifting a little. "I think it best if you get in touch with your MS nurse honey, tell her what's going on and see if she can advise you on what can be done. Are you worried it's a relapse?" Ellie asked in seriousness.

"No...not really. These aren't new symptoms rather an exacerbation of old ones. It will be stress and exhaustion that's triggered it, I know my body well enough. I might need to contact my agent and publisher and ask for a few weeks off after the wedding, just to heal and recharge. I know we can't do a honeymoon until the summer but a couple of weeks of lying on the couch and binge-watching telly is just what is needed, I think" Kate said with a smile, cheered by this new plan.

"Excellent idea, sadly I can't join you, but I'll be around to drop snacks in and turn you every once in a while, to make sure you aren't fusing with the couch" Ellie joked as Kate kicked her with her good leg. "Are you able to walk now?" Ellie asked as she stood up, she gently pulled Kate up who wobbled a little but was standing and able to walk under her own steam, albeit slowly. Ellie led the way to their bedroom, and she grabbed her laptop off the bedside table and sat it between her and Kate as they sat on the couch in their room.

"Why have you brought the laptop?" asked Kate as she propped her legs up on the coffee table and got comfy.

"Wedding music, we better choose some before Aggie has a meltdown over it." Ellie explained as she brought up her music download account.

"Good plan...I had forgotten all about music until she

brought it up this morning. We're shit at this whole being a girl and planning weddings thing, aren't we?" Kate laughed.

"Yeah, honey we really are, thank god Aggie is all over this or else god knows what we would have ended up with." Ellies said with a smile.

"Probably just the two of us at the registry office wearing jeans" Kate guessed, and she was probably bang on the money with that image.

They spent an hour together picking music, it didn't actually take them that long, but they started having fun picking the most inappropriate wedding songs they could think of. The inappropriate wedding list ended up much longer than their proper one and included hits like Beautiful South's 'Don't marry her', Tina Turner's 'What's love got to do with it' and Tammy Wynette's 'D.I.V.O.R.C.E.'

Ellie downloaded their proper music onto a flash drive but kept the alternative songs on a separate flash drive. Kate looked curiously at her, and she explained. "Every time I hear those songs from now on, I'll think back to this moment, and it will make me smile. I want to be able to keep that feeling." Ellie said as she kissed Kate softly.

"You big softie, but make sure you don't mix them up. I don't think the headline of our wedding day should be 'mother of the bride attacks bride with a clipboard'" Kate said with a laugh as they got up.

"Good point, we better start to get ready for this rehearsal. Will you take your stick tonight?...Please?" Ellie asked as she heard noises coming from upstairs that indicated everyone was back in.

"I will, I don't fancy another wobble after today, and

you're right. If Selma can look gorgeous with a stick, then so can I" Kate said with a wink.

Chapter 21

The rehearsal at Oran Mor was to be a simple walk through of the service and where everyone was to stand. Aggie was in full military planning mode as she dragged Gavin by the sleeve up to the front to his correct position as best man. Val was seated in the second row of chairs on the left side of the aisle, she was obviously still in a foul mood as she sat in stony silence, refusing to talk to anyone. Thankfully this appeared to suit almost everyone else, so they left her to it, although Peggy kept giving her dirty looks every once in a while. Clearly Peggy hadn't forgiven her for what she said about Ellie. The Humanist Celebrant arrived and stood up at the front and made his introductions. He had a look of a rugby player about him, he looked solid as he shook hands with everyone.

"Hello there, I'm Stephen Simms, I'll be the celebrant on your special day. Tonight, is just a wee dry run to make sure we all know what we're doing. So where are our witnesses first?" he looked around as Peggy and Ann stepped forward. "Excellent, ladies you will walk in ahead of the bridesmaids and take your place up behind this young man." He pointed towards Gavin. "Bridesmaids?" he then asked as Rachel and Mhairi stepped forward. "Lovely, lovely" he beamed "you ladies will start to make your way down the aisle once the music kicks in and finally the brides?" he looked expectantly as Ellie and Kate walked forward holding hands.

"Lovely, now have you decided how you want to do this? Are you doing the giving away thing or walking yourselves down the aisle? I'm all for tradition myself but more people are opting for the latter."

"Yeah, well they're not" grumbled Bill as he too stepped forward, Seb alongside him. "We'll be walking them down the aisle."

"Of course, excellent choice" Stephen said with a smile. "Ok let's have a run through, places everyone" he shouted like a set director.

The music started to play (thankfully the correct flash drive) as Peggy and Ann walked elegantly down the aisle and took their places at the front. Ellie could hear muttering coming from Val as Peggy walked past her and she noticed the tightening of Peggy's fists. 'Oh Oh…this won't be good' Ellie thought as she continued to keep an eye on them. Next Mhairi and Rachel walked down the aisle and Ellie caught the expression of love on Gavin's face as he watched his wife walk down and turn to face him. She winked at him as she turned to her place.

"We're up love" Bill said as he took his daughter's arm and marched down the aisle in regimental fashion. "Dad, slow down, we aren't riding into battle!" Ellie hissed as he slowed his pace a little. "Sorry love, nerves." he explained as he walked her to her position and then he sat next to Aggie in the front row. Ellie heard Val herself this time she was muttering something along the lines of 'no breeding that family'. Thankfully Bill had missed this little drip of poison and he was smiling benignly at her. Peggy had heard her though and Ellie saw her jaw twitch as she clenched her teeth together in fury. Finally, Kate and Seb made their way down the aisle. Seb was walking slowly, a firm grip on his sister's arm as she walked confidently with her stick, her eyes never leaving Ellie's as she made her way towards her. Ellie had never been so at peace in her whole life, it was as if time stood still in that moment. Kate stood before her, and they just kept looking at each other before a cough brought them round.

"Ahem...may I proceed?" Stephen asked as he looked at them both. They both nodded and smiled as they turned towards him to begin the ceremony practice.

Everything went smoothly until Stephen got to the part about anyone having any objections. He wasn't expecting any, so he started to continue with the rest of his proclamation when he heard a large tut coming from the audience.

"I'm sorry...has someone got something they want to say?" he asked, clearly this had never happened to him before. He looked a little startled as Val stood up, glaring at the room.

"Yes, I do have something to say...how can you stand here and let this sham continue?" Val directed this at Aggie, but Peggy had heard enough, she marched down from her position and bodily lifted Val out of her chair and stomped away dragging her out the door with her. Peggy returned looking flushed but happier now that Val was gone.

“Sorry young man, please continue” she directed at Stephen as she resumed her position. Stephen was obviously startled by the turn the evening was taking but he soldiered on and finished the ceremony without any further hitch.

“I don’t know about the rest of you…but I could do with a drink after that. Shall we head downstairs to the bar?” Stephen said jovially and everyone assented and followed him down to the main bar. Val was nowhere to be seen, no one was sad about her absence and the whole evening took on rather a party atmosphere after that.

Chapter 22

The next morning Ellie was back in the office, her team around her as they had a briefing.

"Kent did we get any information from the chemist...Melanie Stokes?" Ellie asked as she leafed through paperwork in front of her.

"No Ma'am, Mrs Stokes said she didn't see or hear anything out of the ordinary during the day and she had no reason to go out the back until closing time as it was her usual routine to take the rubbish out with her as she locked up." Kent said as she read from Melanie's statement.

"Great" muttered Ellie. "Has anyone found any witnesses?" she asked the room, but no response came forward. Ellie was frustrated and Gavin could see that, so he started with his information hoping to get his boss out of her gloom.

"Doc has more information on the murder weapon. She

says it's definitely metal and not wood, it's also a galvanised metal as she could find no rust particles adhering to the wounds. She's also done some preliminary tests on the amount of force it would have taken to inflict the fatal blow. According to the Doc it wouldn't have taken much strength to carry out these killings…in fact she said anyone relatively able-bodied could have swung the weapon hard enough to kill."

"Even better…so what we have is nothing?" Ellie asked in dismay. She stood up and started pacing in front of the board, she was studying the areas in which each victim was found. It was then that she noticed that Kent had added the locations of the other murders too. Ellie stopped and looked closely at the locations. An idea suddenly came to her, and it lit her face up instantly. She turned back to her team with a glint in her eye.

"We need to look for patterns, it's the only evidence left to us right now. My first question to you all is, who has most reason to kill drug dealers?"

"Junkies that owe them money?" Harris suggested.

"Yes, but junkies usually owe money to maybe one or two dealers…not every single one in the area. Who else?" Ellie asked.

"What about a vigilante? Trying to clean up the area?" offered Gavin and Ellie could tell that his mind was firmly on the cocoon patrol when he said this.

"It's a distinct possibility Gav, especially now we know that it doesn't need much strength to carry out these attacks. My only reservation about this line of thought is that the first person attacked in this manner was not a dealer, it was one of the vigilantes." Ellie reminded him but she wasn't unconvinced of the group being involved in this. "Anyone else?" Ellie asked but her team just looked back at her.

"How about the families of addicts" she said to them. "Look at the positions of the attacks...do you notice what is bang in the middle of all of these places? The community Centre...where a group of addicts families meet up a couple of times a week." Ellie finished as all eyes started to brighten in comprehension.

"Well bugger me, how did we not spot that" muttered Gavin.

"We didn't have this information until now Gav, we never thought to look at it, but each of the murders occur no more than half a mile in any direction from the Community Centre. I think we need to talk to the members of that group, see if you can get a list of members before we start asking questions." Ellie said to Kent as a phone rang in the office. They were discussing details when Harris called out to her.

"Ma'am...there's been another one!"

"Oh god, Kent get on that list as a matter of urgency, the rest of you with me." Ellie barked as they ran out of the station.

Chapter 23

Ryan's body was found lying near the goalposts of the football pitch near the flats. Doc Brett's tent was already around the body. Frost lay lightly on the grass as Gavin stamped his feet a little to keep them warm as he took a call. Harris, who had been talking to a local PC walked over, still writing notes as she did.
"Ma'am, Ryan was found by a dog walker about an hour ago, apparently it gave her quite a turn, they've had to take her to hospital with chest pains."

"What about the dog?" Gavin asked as he looked around but spotted no puppies. He looked disappointed as he hung up his phone.

"It's been dropped off with the witness's daughter. Uniform got her statement before she went to hospital, saw no one. She let her dog off the lead to play fetch, she does this every morning. The dog ran straight to Ryan's body and barked like mad, but she swears he didn't touch the body."

"Good, Gav, let's see what the Doc says. Harris, the usual drill, get uniform and start knocking on doors at the flats, see if anyone saw anything. I want you to find Ryan's next of kin details, take family liaison with you and notify them, will you?" Ellie asked as she put covers on her shoes and gloves on before she stepped under the tape.

"Yes Ma'am. I have his mother's address here; I'll go now before she hears another way." And at that, Harris walked back towards the uniformed officers and started organising them to their tasks.

Inside the tent, Ellie saw Ryan's body for the first time. He was even younger looking in death. He was lying face down with a wound in the back of his head. He was wearing the same clothes that he had on when he was arrested yesterday.

"Gav, when was he released?"

"He was bailed and released at 8.00 last night, that was the phone call I was making." He explained.

"Good thinking big guy" Ellie said as she looked at Ryan. "What have you got so far Doc?"

"According to body temp, I would say he died not long after 10 last night. He has a similar blow to the head as the others, but I would need to examine him in better detail to give you a positive match Ellie. But I can see one difference…he has defensive wounds."

"Really? Where?" Ellie looked on with interest as Doc lifted his right hand, it was bruised and cut.

"So, he got a couple of hits in then?" Gav asked and Doc nodded.

"Yes, I believe that he managed to strike his murderer with some force. They will be marked from it if his knuckles are in this state."

"Is there any chance of the killers DNA being on his hands?" Ellie asked hopefully.

"There's a possibility, but it rained again last night so don't get your hopes up." Doc cautioned. "Forensics have also had a search of the body under my supervision. They found this in his socks." Doc Brett produced an evidence bag from her kit. It contained rolled up bank notes and what was unmistakably little bags of heroin.

"Ryan…where did you get this lot so quickly?" Ellie muttered. "The boy was only out of Maryhill for at most two hours before he was killed. He must have gone straight to his supplier on his way back!"

"He would have needed to, we confiscated what we found on him earlier in the day. He must have already done at least one deal though; he had no money when he left the station as we confiscated that too." Gavin said as he looked down at the young man and Ellie could tell he was thinking once again of his brother at that age.

"Right, we can't put it off any longer, we need to go see that support group and see what they know. Doc will you call me if you find anything?"

"You're in my speed dial Ellie, I'll let you know" Doc said with a smile as she went back to examining Ryan.

"First thing to look for at this group is a black eye Gav" Ellie said as they walked off towards their cars.

Chapter 24

When they arrive at the centre, by luck, the group has just broken for tea. The group are huddled in little clusters around a table full of sandwiches. Val is there handing them out and Doreen is sat on a stool pouring cups of tea, as Ellie approached Val saw her and walked into the kitchen and slammed the door.
"Nice welcome" muttered Gavin as they stopped at Doreen.

"Never mind her hen, she's always been rubbish with apologies, and I believe you are due one" Doreen said kindly. "Now what can I do for you?"

"We need to find out more about the people who attend this group regularly. Is there a signup sheet or anything that you could give me?" asked Ellie.

"I'm not sure if there's a sheet of names or anything but, if it helps, I know everyone here and I'll happily give you details if you need them, but it would be up to the group leader, that's him in the turtleneck jumper, Sid his name is. Lovely man, but aye if you ask him then it should be fine." At that Doreen got gingerly off her chair and winced as she grabbed her crutch.

"Are you ok?" Ellie asked as the older woman started to move off slowly.

"Aye I'm fine hen, I'm waiting on an operation on my hip, some days it's more painful than others but there's no use complaining is there?" she smiled a little and hobbled off to the kitchen to help Val.

Ellie and Gavin head towards Sid who was a young man attempting to grow a beard…unsuccessfully. Patches of hair like tufts sprouted from his chin.

"Sid? I'm Detective Superintendent McVey and this is DI Bickerton. We are hoping you will be able to give us some information that could help a current enquiry."

"Of course, what can I do to help? Is it these killings? Awful business…but…um…I've heard that the young men killed were involved in drugs…is that correct?" he asked quietly.

"How did you hear that, Sid?" asked Gavin as they hadn't mentioned drugs in any press reports.

"Oh, someone will have mentioned it in passing, the rumour mill and all that" he laughed nervously "anyway, how can I help you?"

"We need the names of anyone who would regularly attend this meeting." Ellie said quietly as she didn't want the rest of the group to hear.

"You can't think anyone here would do such a thing?" Sid

looked scandalised so Ellie decided on a little white lie.

“No Sid not at all, we just think that the best people to help in situations such as this would be a victim support group, I mean they will know more about it than we will, eh?” she gave him a winning smile that seemed to pacify him a bit.

“Well yes of course, our little group has had some bad dealings with pushers over the years…I’m sure the people here would love to give you the benefit of their experience.” He turned away and clapped loudly “Everyone can you please form a discussion circle, this lady wants to chat to you all” Sid smiled back, pleased at his idea but Ellie wasn’t expecting this.

“Sid, I meant for us to discuss it privately, not have a group session” she whispered harshly. Sid realised his mistake and flushed but didn’t seem able to admit his error and just smiled.

“Nonsense, this is the best way, out in the open so that everyone gets the information first-hand. It’s how we do things here” he said with maddening smugness as he turned to get chairs.

“And that’s how he knows its dealers being killed…first-hand information in the group” muttered Ellie to Gavin and he nodded. A circle of expectant faces watched them closely as they took their seats beside Sid.

“Everyone these are policemen…er…police people?” Sid suddenly confused himself before carrying on. They want our help and expertise to find out what happened to those drug deaths” there was a murmur of conversation after this, and Ellie took it as approval to carry on before Sid made his role any bigger.

"Thank you everyone, we promise not to take up too much of your time, but we were hoping that if we give you some names, would you be able to tell us anything about them?" Ellie hoped this would be the quickest way to determine who here knows anything. "First of all, can we start with Kai Neilson, anyone have any information on him?" she looked around expectantly as a man stood up, he was large in his fifties and angry.

"Aye…that wee toerag sold my Alison the drugs that killed her…she overdosed on New Year's Eve 2 years ago." He said gruffly.

"That's Pete" came a whisper behind Ellie that made her jump. Doreen had sat her chair down quietly behind them. "Peter Moir, he's a joiner, he's married and has a son and poor Alison." Ellie nodded and noted that down as Pete was still mouthing off about Kai.

"Thank you" Ellie interrupted him "This is really useful information, once I get around all of you would you mind if I chatted to you more about him?" Pete nodded curtly and then sat down, the woman beside him patted his arm gently.

"Next would be Ryan Summerhill…" Ellie left it open.

"We know he sold drugs to a young teenager this week." said Sid but apart from this, no one else had anything to say about him.

"Ok…what about Michael or Mick Adams?"

"He sold my niece Ketamine…she fell off a bridge…god know why she was trying to climb it…she fell…she's in a wheelchair now." A small woman said quietly, tears in her eyes. She was tearing a tissue to shreds in her lap as she told the story of the hardships now faced by her family.

Doreen leaned in once more "That's Jean Robinson, her niece Karen was only 17 at the time."

"Thank you for telling us Jean…next we have David Sharpe; he was killed 6 months ago." Ellie explained.

"Here" a young man raised his hand, he was built like Gavin, tattoos covering his arms. "He was my wee sister's boyfriend. I hated him…he got her hooked on heroin…we tried to help her, but she wouldn't listen…she ran away with him when she was 16. He put her out to work on the streets to pay for her habit…knocked her about…she killed herself 3 years ago…she was only 19. I never found Dave…if I had I would have killed him with my bare hands for what he did to my family. My mother has never got over it…never will" he said quietly but rage and grief still filled him.

"That was Andy Livingston, he works at a women's addiction centre…one of the only men allowed in the whole of Glasgow." Doreen volunteered.

"You are all being very helpful, and I thank you for your candour…next name is Steven Webber." Ellie looked around and an older woman raised her hand.

"My son supposedly owed him money…he jumped him coming home from college on night and beat him severely. My boy hasn't left the house in over 18 months, he's too scared. He gave up college and all his friends, he just sits in a dark room watching telly now." She said with a tear running down her cheek.

"Sally McCusker, her son Aiden is agoraphobic since his attack" came Doreen's voice from behind.

"Thank you Sally…finally we have Graham McAndrew." Ellie looked up but was met with silence. Everyone was looking around nervously but said nothing. Ellie looked back towards Doreen, and she looked sad as she said, "I thought you would have known that one hen...Graham McAndrew killed Val's son."

Chapter 25

Ellie and Gavin were both sitting in the car outside the community centre. What had been said in there had left them reeling.

"Did you know?" asked Gavin quietly.

"No...Val's never said, and I don't remember anyone else talking about Val's family life." Ellie's mind was reeling.

"Val couldn't have done this though Els, she has an alibi for Kai's death and for last night, she was at the rehearsal." Gavin said, trying to find positives in this mess.

"I don't think she has Gav...her alibi for Kai is that she was sleeping. Doreen said she was asleep and then woke to find Val sleeping too. Val could easily have slipped out unnoticed and then returned before Doreen woke up."

"She could have...would have been a hell of a risk though...anyway what about last night?" said Gavin.

"She left early Gav, remember she had a row with Peggy and left. She had plenty of time if she got a taxi outside

Oran Mor. Shit...what the hell am I going to do?" she muttered and closed her eyes, suddenly exhausted from the day. Gavin sat quietly; he knew Ellie's brain was in overdrive, so he waited to see what she came up with. After a few moments her eyes opened again, focused and alert.

"Right, I want you to go back to the office and divide the list of group members between yourself, Kent and Harris. I want every one of them checked but focus on those who spoke up in the group about having dealings with our murder victims. I want their movements on each murder night checked and validated as much as possible. I'll drop you off on my way." She said as she started the engine.

"Are you going to speak to Kate?" he asked.

"No...I'm going to talk to Peggy. Kate has a lot on her mind right now, I'm not adding to her stress until I have to. Peggy will have the information, probably more than anyone else in the family. I'll know what I need to do once I talk to her." Ellie said decisively.

"You think you're going to have to arrest Val, don't you?" Gavin said, worried.

"It's a possibility...think Gav...if she wasn't Kate's aunt and you had the information in front of you...what would you do?" she asked calmly, her eyes focused on the road.

"You're right...I would pull her in. I hope this doesn't cause you family problems Els"

"So do I" she muttered.

Chapter 26

Ellie waited in the park for Peggy, she had decided that this conversation was best had away from the house, so she sent Peggy an emergency message that they needed to talk and gave her location. She was watching the swans on the river Kelvin as she stamped her feet to warm them up a little. Her mind was reeling with information, what was she going to do if Kate's auntie was a serial killer? She was running through all the evidence in her head, preoccupied she didn't hear Peggy approach, she jumped a little when Peggy touched her elbow.

"Sorry young'un, I didn't mean to startle you. I did call your name, what's wrong?" Peggy got straight to the point as she knew Ellie wouldn't have called for this chat if there wasn't something serious going on.

"Peggy…I need you to tell me everything you know about what happened to Val's son." Ellie said quietly as they found a bench to sit down.

"Colin? Why do you need to know about that?"

"Please Peggy…it's important." Ellie didn't want to give any more details until she heard the story. Peggy nodded, understanding that this was urgent, so she began to describe what she knew.

"Well Colin was Val's only child, she spoiled him rotten. I didn't know the lad all that well, as you know we haven't been close through the years. I know that Val and her husband spent a lot of money on private education for Colin, all for nothing I'm afraid as he was lazy, he failed every exam and left school with no qualifications and his parents up to their eyes in debt. Val's husband was frustrated as he wanted Colin to go into a trade, but Val was having none of it, he was too sensitive and artistic according to her. Anyway, Colin lived with his parents until the day he died. He was working as a security guard, protecting building sites in the city centre. Apparently one night just before Christmas, think it was the 21st, he was working that night when some teenagers broke in. They were either there to steal or there to deal drugs as both ecstasy and power tools were found on them later. So, Colin spotted them on the CCTV from his hut and he went out to chase them. One of them had a knife…they stabbed him in the chest and ran off. CCTV didn't catch the assault but did catch the boys running off. Colin was left to die; he was found by the day shift when they arrived at 7 o'clock the following morning."

"God that's awful" muttered Ellie. "What happened to the lads that did it?" Ellie asked but she knew that Graham McAndrew was not in jail as he was murdered this year.

"Well, the local police were able to identify the lads from

the CCTV, something to do with what they were wearing, they had been stopped earlier that night and cautioned and were all wearing distinctive bomber jackets with a smiley face on them. Anyway, the police pay a visit to each of the boys and find the drugs and stolen equipment at their homes. They didn't ever find the knife though. They went to trial but with no prints, no murder weapon, and no witnesses, they received a not proven judgement on the murder but were found guilty of burglary. Each of them did a minimum amount of time...months at best I think and then they were back on streets. By the look on your face, this isn't what you wanted to hear?" Peggy asked as Ellie rubbed her face with her hands, unsure of what to do.

"Yeah, you could say that, Peggy. It looks like this series of murders I'm investigating has something to do with the support group that Val is involved with. Every one of the victims has affected the life in a negative way of a member of that group...including Val." Ellie explained.

"Alibi?" Peggy asked.

"Not a rock solid one" Ellie admitted. "I have to treat her as a suspect Peggy. Do you think her capable?"

"I'd like to say no...for your sake and for Katie's...but Colin was her world...I don't think there's much she wouldn't do for him" Peggy admitted.

"Shit" groaned Ellie.

"Is she the only suspect?"
"No, there are a few members of the group that have motive...I've got the team working on whether or not they had the opportunity."

"If that's the case...I would suggest you don't do anything

about Val just now, get more information, narrow down your suspect list further. There's no point upsetting the family until you know more."

"You think this will upset Kate and Aggie?" Ellie asked, she had been dreading that.

"Not in the way you think, Aggie will feel upset for Kate, Kate in turn will be upset for you. Neither of the two will be upset for Val. Just keep going Ellie, you'll find the truth one way or another and then you let the justice system make the finals decisions. It's all you can do." Peggy said as she patted Ellie's arm and got up.

"Thanks Peggy…can you not tell the others yet? Not until I know for sure…"

"I won't say a word; but keep me up to date…just so that I can be prepared for the fallout and also keep Val at a relative distance if needs be."

"Of course…thanks again Peggy. I better go back to work."

"Indeed, and I'm needed back at yours…I need to keep young Seb from burying Aggie's clipboard in the garden… and potentially her with it. Good luck Ellie." Peggy turned away and walked back towards the house. Ellie watched her go for a moment, grateful for Peggy's insights. She hoped that she wouldn't need her to protect the family from potentially a serial killer in their midst.

Chapter 27

Back in the office, Ellie calls the team together for a meeting. Everyone looks tired, Ellie feels tired herself, but they needed to push ahead.

"OK boys and girls what have we got, in regard to alibis for the people in the support group?" Ellie asked as she perched herself on her desk.

"Ma'am, as far as we can tell, all but two people have alibis for all of the nights in question. Two members of the group either don't have any alibi or don't have strong alibis..." Kent hesitated, looking furtively at Ellie who understood.

"One of them being Val, I take it?" Kent nodded. "That's ok Kent...I had expected as much. Who is the other person?"

"Peter Moir, the man whose daughter died of an overdose. He says he was at work for two of the murders and at home on his own for the others. The problem is that he's a self-employed electrician...no boss to check with that he was indeed working."

"Good work everyone Ellie said as she got up and wrote Val's name and Peter's on the murder board.

"These two people must now be considered our main persons of interest. I want both of them brought in for questioning. Obviously, I can't interview Val so Gavin would you do the honours?" Gavin nodded and Ellie stopped in front of the board deep in thought for a moment. "Something still bothers me...I hate when there's an irregularity...Eric. Why if your whole purpose is revenge on drug dealers, why do you hit an old man? Harris, I want you to look into Eric's life, leave no stone unturned. I want to know if there is anything in his past that would make sense of this. This could be a late one folks so please call childminders or spouses and apologise on my behalf, I'll order the pizzas in...let's get to work.

Chapter 28

"What are you playing at dragging me out of my house at this hour?" thundered Val as Gavin walked into the interview room. "And where is Eleanor? Is this her doing? Poisonous little madam, after the family money"

"Enough!" bellowed Gavin as he sat down, he was beyond his limit with Val now. "You're here because there are some questions, we need to ask you on the record. Detective Superintendant McVey cannot conduct the interview for obvious reasons."

"What obvious reasons? Has she been caught doing something dodgy? Wouldn't put it past her...she's got shifty eyes that one...bet there's some gypsy blood in there..."

"One more word and I'll charge you under the Hate Crimes Act. Now my first question is, why do you volunteer at the community centre?" he asked, attempting to calm himself. This question seemed to throw Val off her vindictive stride.

"Oh...well one must do their bit for the local community." sniffed Val, now suddenly as pious as a bishop. "Those of us who are Christian minded should do good works." Gavin looked down at her hands to check for stigmata. Val was the most un-Christian person he's ever met...and he had met a cannibal.

"Why do you particularly do your charitable works with families of addicts?"

"Because addicts tear families apart, those poor people need my help."

"I see...nothing to do with what happened to Colin?" Gavin asked gently. Val went pale and her eyes narrowed.

"Eleanor has been gossiping with that Peggy I see. I'm surprised you need to ask me questions, no doubt you know all about it. They killed my boy and got away with it, he was just doing his job...that scum got away with it."

"Not really...Graham McAndrew didn't, he's dead...didn't you know?"

"I didn't know...but good riddance." Val said quietly but with cold eyes.

"He died on the 27th of August of this year; do you happen to know where you were on the night of the 27th?" Gavin asked as casually as he could.

"How am I supposed to remember that far back? I've no idea where I was... Oh I get it! You think I've done it. I'm an old woman, pick on someone else to be Eleanor's scapegoat."

"This is not about scapegoating; I'm simply asking if you

know where you were on the night the lad that killed your son was murdered."

"I've no idea where I was, what does it matter anyway? Surely all these drug pushers were killed by the same person, yes? I have alibis, I was with Doreen when that little thug Neilson boy was killed."

"Who was asleep" Gavin reminded her "And you left the rehearsal early enough to have committed another of the attacks…can you tell me what you did once you left Oran Mor?"

"I got a taxi home and went to bed."

"Did you see anyone?"

"The taxi driver" she said sarcastically. "I don't know… maybe Bobby might have saw me come home, he's usually on lookout at that time of the night."

"We'll check that out, you got the taxi at the rank outside Oran Mor?" Gavin asked and Val nodded. "For the benefit of the tape can you answer?" he said.

"Yes" Val said through gritted teeth.

"Thank you, now finally I would like to ask you to submit to a body search with a female officer." Gavin asked, Val looked as though he had asked her to go in a window in Amsterdam.

"A body search?" she screeched as she clutched her chest melodramatically.

"Yes…one of the victims managed to hit their killer, we want to check you for bruises." Gavin said coldly having had enough of the dramatics.

"What if I don't agree?"

"Well, you could...but then we would think you have something to hide...and we would get a warrant anyway." Seeing no way out of this Val agreed and was taken to an examination room.

Ellie was in the next room with Peter Moir, she had heard some of Val's complaining from the hallway and was glad not to be dealing with her. Peter was sitting placidly across the table from her, calm and open.

"Mr Moir, we are interviewing members of your group in connection with a series of murders, one of which as you know is the man who you blame for your daughter's death. I hope you understand why we need to ascertain your whereabouts on the evenings in question."

"Aye I understand, I'm glad they're dead...I'm not gonna lie about that hen but I never did it, I would be no use to my missus if I was in Barlinnie would I?"

"Very true, now you told my officers that you were at work...is there anyone that can vouch for you?" Peter thought for a moment before answering.

"Aye possibly...a lot of times when I'm called to a job, they need a plumber too, so my mate Rab is usually called too. Now I'm not sure if this happened on those particular nights, but you can ask him. He keeps better records than I do."

"OK, what's Rab's full name and I'll get in touch."

"Robert Laird, here take my phone, his number is in there." Peter says as he hands over his phone with the contact details and Ellie makes a note of it.

"Thank you for that, hopefully he can narrow down your activities for us and you can be removed from our list.

One final thing Mr Moir, if you wouldn't mind? Would you be willing to submit to a body search? We believe the last victim got a punch in and would have left a mark."

"Aye, I've got nothing to hide." And before Ellie could direct him to follow her to find a male officer, he had whipped off his shirt and joggers and was standing in his boxers. Not bruises anywhere on him. Ellie also looked at his hands, no defensive wounds there either. She cleared her throat "um…thank you Mr Moir, if you wouldn't mind getting re-dressed, I'll be back in a moment."

Ellie left the room quickly and spotted Gavin walking up the corridor towards her.

"Val's got no bruises but also no alibi as yet, need to track down a taxi driver, how did yours go?"

"No bruises and a potential alibi, a plumber named Rab who he usually does jobs with. Also, Moir's a big bloke, I think if he struck you in anger with something, there would be much more damage. I think it's someone weaker."

"Back to Val then?" Gavin said.

"I just don't know…we've got nothing to hold either of them for now…release them both, we'll keep going." Ellie decided as she walked back towards the office.

Chapter 29

Ellie gathered the team once more, a little deflated from the interviews. She had hoped things would be clearer for her, but they ended up more muddled in her head.

"Does anyone have anything?" Ellie asked through her hands as she rubbed at her face. "Any witnesses in the Mews?"

"Ma'am a woman was out feeding a lame fox at about 10.30pm. She said she heard an argument coming from the pitches, a man and a woman she said." Harris answered.

"Could be our victim and Val? Could be a couple having a row? It's not enough...Harris what have you got on Eric?"

"I pulled some strings with a mate of mine, I got hold of his military record about half an hour ago. He joined the army at 18 but left his first regiment under something of a cloud." Harris began.

"Really? What were the circumstances?" Ellie asked as she perked up a little.

"He was implicated in the death of a young Corporal. According to the files, the Corporal was found dead after what appeared to be an overdose. Another soldier accused Eric of being the one who sold the drugs. An investigation was launched but nothing was ever proven. Eric was transferred to the Fusiliers shortly after the investigation was completed. After that he appears to have been a model soldier, retired on a full pension after 25 years. No criminal record after leaving the army." Harris finished.

"It's a link though, another drug dealer punished perhaps?" Ellie pondered.

"They must have a long memory Ma'am, all the rest are current dealers, why go after a man who hasn't done anything illegal in over 30 years?" Harris asked.

"Because it's personal." Ellie said. "Kent dig deeper into this, I want details on the solider that died, I want his next of kin and anything else you can find. This matters to someone. Harris get on to the alibis for Val and Peter Moir, I need to know if they are still viable suspects. Work on these tomorrow folks, anything turns up please contact Gavin as I will be busy" she said with a smile as the team laughed.

"Oh, that reminds us Ma'am" Kent said cheerfully as she bent down behind her desk and picked up a gift bag "this is from all of us, we hope your day goes well and congratulations" they all cheered, and Ellie smiled.

"Thank you, you're a good bunch…and yes you're all still invited to the night do where I will be buying you all a round of drinks." Cheers met this and Ellie said goodnight and left the office.

Chapter 30

Ellie walked through the door of her home and was greeted enthusiastically by Bruiser, she hadn't seen much of the little guy lately, so she bent down to give him a good belly rub, his tail beating a samba against the floor. Only when she stood up did she notice Kate sitting in the semi darkness watching her, Bella asleep on her lap.

"Hi honey, what are you doing sitting in the dark?" Ellie asked as she put a lamp on, she got a good look at Kate's face, and she looked troubled. "What's wrong?"

"Val's been on the phone." Kate said in explanation and Ellie nodded her understanding.

"Cursing my name by any chance?" Ellie asked as she dropped down beside Kate on the couch.

"You could say that she says you're trying to frame her for murder to get hold of my money" Kate said as she rolled her eyes. "You want to tell me what's actually going on?"

"We brought her in for questioning today, no because I'm framing her but because the evidence led me to her. I've got a bunch of dead drug dealers, all with links to the family support group that Val is a member of. Then we find out that one of the murder victims actually killed Val's son." Ellie explained.

"Colin? I didn't know he was murdered...I was young when he died...poor Val." Kate said quietly.

"We've interviewed the group members, and all have alibis except for one man and Val. We're chasing down people who they think might have seen them on certain nights, a taxi driver in Val's case. Once we know this then we can move forward." Ellie said, keeping her eyes on Kate for any hints of anger but she found only love and understanding.

"I take it you didn't tell me because you didn't want me to worry?"

"Yes...you're in the middle of an M.S. flareup and dealing with a wedding, I didn't want to add to the stress until I was sure."

"Do you think she did it?" Kate asked quietly.

"Honestly? I don't know. You've known her all your life... what do you think?"

"I'm not sure Ellie, she was in and out of my life when I was young...she could be cold and cruel at times. But I don't know if she would be capable of murder. Mum and Peggy are coming over...I called them after Val phoned me. Maybe they would know more than me." They cuddled together on the couch, enjoying the comfort of closeness. Ellie breathed in the scent of Kate's perfume as her body relaxed. She had no idea how long they sat in silence, but they didn't move until Aggie and Peggy walked through the door. Aggie went straight to Kate and gave her a hug. Peggy squeezed Ellie's arm, "We need to tell you something, it's something that we've not spoken about in 25 years...but it's time." Peggy said as she looked at Aggie who nodded but who kept her eyes locked on Kate.

"You know how Val acts? she looks down on people and acts like Lady of the manor?" Kate and Ellie nodded so Peggy continued. "Val's family were dirt poor; I know you know a bit of this Katie but not the whole thing...your grandmother worked herself half to death as a cleaner not because your grandad died young...but because he was jailed for triple murder and hanged. He killed a man who he had an argument with at work... and tried to cover the crime by setting the house on fire, he didn't realise that the bloke's wife and young son were upstairs... they died in the fire." Peggy stopped as Kate's eyes filled with tears, Aggie clutched at her hand.

"Val inherited his temper...we only realised after your dad did a runner. He owed money to dangerous people and left...Val blamed your mother for him leaving and she arrived round at the house in a fury one night not long after. I was tucking you in, she didn't know I was there. I heard yelling and ran out to find Val beating your mum severely with an umbrella." Peggy said, her eyes ablaze with anger at the memory.

"If Peggy wasn't there that night, I don't know what she would have done. I think the only reason you didn't wake up is because you hadn't been well, so the doctor has given you some medicine to help you sleep." admitted Aggie. "I was hurt on the floor; Peggy threw her out of the house and threatened her with the police if she ever came back...we didn't hear from her for years after that. In fact, it was her husband Norman that calmed the waters... he was a kind man, too good for Val. He wanted to see Katie, missed her he said so we allowed visits again, although always supervised. Val never talked about the incident and never showed that temper towards us again." Aggie finished her story and then hugged Kate once more. Peggy looked towards Ellie "we needed to tell you now because of your case...when you came to me earlier, I knew I should have told you then...but it's Aggie's story... I needed to talk to her first." Peggy explained.

"Thank you for telling me, it doesn't make things any easier though...it takes Val right to the top of the suspect list and unless her alibi checks out...she will be arrested. Do you think she will come to the wedding tomorrow?" Ellie asked.

"Oh of course she will, she will act like nothing has happened, that's her style...speaking of the wedding, Katie get packed, you're staying with me tonight" Aggie said.

"Wait...why?" Kate asked in confusion.

"It's bad luck to see each other before the wedding and I'll be damned if I'm allowing any bad luck to befall this wedding!" Aggie said with feeling. Kate didn't see how she could refuse the request. The next time Ellie would see her, they would be getting married.

Chapter 31

Ellie woke the next morning after a disturbed sleep, her unconscious brain mulling over all that was discussed the night before. She was getting worried about the possibility of having to arrest a family member. Her eyes flew open. "I'm getting married today" she muttered to herself. She turned over and stared at the cold empty place in the bed where Kate should have been, she hated waking up without her, it didn't feel right. Her bedroom door flung open, and Gavin walked in carrying a suit bag which he deposited on the chair in the corner before he jumped onto the bed and started bouncing Ellie up and down.

"It's your wedding day mate! Why are you still in bed, shouldn't you be doing stuff?" he said, still bouncing.

"Like what?" Ellie grumbled as she tried to kick him off the bed, but he dodged her foot.

"I dunno...girl stuff. Mhairi is already over at Peggy's for hair and makeup, who's doing yours?" he asked.

"I'm not wearing makeup, and I'll just straighten my hair and I'll be good to go." Ellie said simply, she hated having to anything more than that to herself.

"Over my dead body" Gavin screeched looking horror stricken. "The lovely Kate is at this very moment getting plucked, preened and blow-dried in order to look her best for you. You are not showing me up by turning up like you're going to work!" At this point if Gavin had been wearing pearls, he would be clutching them.

"You are such a sweetie wife sometimes, when did you turn into my mother?" she said jokingly but the cough from the door stopped her in her tracks. She looked up to find Ann standing there looking none too pleased herself.

"Well as your aunt and the woman who raised you, I agree with him now you just march yourself into that shower Eleanor McVey and then I'm going to sort your hair and makeup, and don't you dare even think of arguing with me today!" warned Ann as she turned to leave. Once Ann was gone Ellie slapped Gavin in the chest.

"I can't believe you got me in trouble!" she whispered.

"You got yourself in trouble" he said as he shoved her back.

"Are there any developments in the case?" Ellie asked.

"Ellie switch your brain off for the day and concentrate on the happiest day of your life, will you? No there are no developments yet, come on let's get some coffee and then you get showered or Ann will kill the pair of us." Gavin warned.

"Good plan, while we're having coffee I can fill you in on what I was told last night." Ellie said as they headed towards the kitchen. Over coffee she told Gavin the story Aggie and Peggy had passed on about Val, Gavin got angrier as the story unfolded.

“The old cow! He growled, how could anyone hurt Aggie like that? And she didn’t report it?”

“No, she didn’t want any more trouble I think…but I have my suspicions that Peggy may have warned Val off from that point.” Ellie said as she drained her cup.

“It explains Peggy’s hatred towards her, I’d rather have Peggy as a friend than a foe” he said as he shuddered at the thought of what Peggy had the power to do should she be vengeful enough.

“Will you two get off your backsides!!” roared Ann and they bolted from the kitchen like scalded cats.

Chapter 32

At Peggy's house wedding preparations were much further ahead. Kate was getting her makeup applied by Rachel and her hair pinned by Mhairi, who stood up straight with a groan as she rubbed at her stomach.

"Are you ok?" asked Kate without moving her lips as Rachel was applying her lipstick.

"Oh, I'm fine, these two are just having a punch up in there I think" quipped Mhairi with a chuckle.

"You better not be dropping those kids today" joked Kate as she had noticed that Mhairi's bump had shifted since she saw her a few days ago.

"I better not be! I hope to have a good time today and eat my bodyweight in those wee mini burgers your mum has ordered from the caterer, so I promise, even if my waters break, I'll cross my legs until tomorrow." Mhairi laughed as she held her hand up in solemn oath before continuing to rub her stomach. Kate turned and spotted Rachel watching Mhairi carefully.

"Are you and Seb thinking about kids?" Kate asked her gently. Rachel smiled, a tear forming in her eyes, and she nodded.

"We started the adoption process before we came over, we weren't sure if we would be accepted considering we are not what they would class as a typical family. The case worker we've been dealing with has been lovely, she doesn't see any problems arising so hopefully we might have news soon."

"Aw Rachel that's amazing!" screeched Kate as she grabbed her hand.

"I know...don't say anything to your mum yet though... Seb wants to surprise her when we know for sure."

"I won't say a thing...she will be so pleased, finally getting grandkids to fuss over." Kate said smiling.

"You never know, you could have some too" Rachel said as she continued with the makeup.

"Nope, that isn't in our future, we had that discussion pretty early on. I've never wanted to have kids and Ellie's career is her world, so it's up to you two to carry on the family line...no pressure" Kate said with a chuckle.

Aggie bustled in just then, dressed but without her hat, she had earbuds in and was threatening the florist with dismemberment, in fact she made a note on her clipboard as if the violence had been pencilled in. Peggy arrived at her back, dressed and with her hat on. She looked almost regal as she swept through elegantly, she was carrying a tray of champagne flutes.

"Bucks Fizz everyone" she announced as she passed a

glass to everyone and an orange juice to Mhairi who took it with a sigh.

"I'm close to sending these two an eviction notice, no alcohol, chronic heartburn and I keep getting stuck in the bath" she muttered under her breath as Peggy chuckled.

Peggy raised her glass "To Katie and Ellie…I hope you both will be very happy together…enjoy your day my dear" she said simply before lifting the glass to her lips and draining the lot. Kate didn't miss as Peggy turned, that there were tears in her eyes.

Aggie ended her call having missed this touching moment and she looked around. "What are you all doing just sitting about? Katherine, get dressed or you'll be late." Kate rolled her eyes but stood up, best not arguing with Aggie when she was still in organisation mode. She hoped that Ellie was having a calmer morning.

Chapter 33

Ellie and Gavin were at Oran Mor greeting guests as they trickled in, Ann had forced Ellie into a chair and put subtle makeup on her despite her protests and had even managed, with Gavin as an assistant, to get Ellie's hair into an elegant French plait. It was all they were able to get the squirming woman to sit for. Bill wandered up to his daughter and put his arm around her and smiled.

"I can't believe this day has finally come…I always hoped that you would find someone to make you happy. Kate is a lovely young woman and smart as a whip…your gran would have loved her." He said gently and Ellie filled up. He hugged her once more and then went to find Ann, he knew Ellie needed to put herself back together.

Liz Aitken and her husband arrived as Ellie composed herself.

"Hi Ellie, wow who forced you into some makeup?" Liz said, impressed. "See if I wasn't married to this one, I'd marry you myself" she joked as she hugged her friend. "You look lovely, I hope it's a good day for you. Come on you" she grabbed her husband's hand "we better find some good seats. See you on the other side Els" she said with a smile as they went off to get seated.

A taxi pulled up and a rowdy bunch got out, once they say Ellie, they roared her name and cheered as they ran towards her and picked her up in a bear hug. She laughed as she returned the many hugs and handshakes before the crowd obediently went off to find seats. Gavin looked at her as she fixed her suit, her smile radiating.

"Who was that?" he asked, there must have been about six huge men and women in that crowd that he didn't recognise.

"That was my old team at the PSNI" she explained.

"They're huge? What do the PSNI do for recruitment? Lure them down from the hills with a chunk of meat?"

"No" she laughed "They're also the PSNI mixed-sex football team." she said.

They greeted several more guests including Kate's school friends and her publisher who brought a very famous author with her, disguised in dark glasses and a large hat. Kate was a huge fan of the author and her publisher had arranged the visit as a wedding present for her. Finally, Peggy and Aggie showed up and Ellie hugged both of them in turn.

"You both look beautiful" she said with a smile.

"Thank you, Ellie, you've scrubbed up nicely yourself." Peggy said with pride. Aggie was about to say something, but her face flushed as she stared behind Peggy at the guest that just arrived. Everyone turned to see Val walk stiffly through but not before she aimed a self-satisfied smirk in Peggy's direction. It was then that Ellie noticed that Val was wearing the same hat as Peggy, Gavin instinctively walked towards Peggy and gently took her arm and whispered in her ear "she's not worth it, it's your niece's wedding day, don't give her the satisfaction." he muttered over and over as Peggy stared cold hatred towards her but did not retaliate to the obvious provocation. Peggy had been discussing how much she loved her hat and where she got it at the rehearsal. There was no way it was a coincidence Ellie thought as she watched Val smiling triumphantly and sit down.

"I'll get that old cow if it's the last thing I do" Peggy said through barely restrained rage."

"Margaret, don't let her ruin a fine moment in our family history." Aggie said gently as she touched her sister's arm. Peggy closed her eyes and breathed deeply for a few moments. When she opened her eyes again, they were once more filled with the light-hearted joviality that was there before Val's appearance. Ellie took a moment before Kate arrived to grab both women by the hand.

"I want to thank you for welcoming into your family... apart from Ann...you've both felt like mothers to me...I want you to know that I love you both and I appreciate all you have done for us..." This was enough for Aggie as she pulled Ellie into a crushing hug. Ellie returned the hug for a while before she spoke once more. "Um...Aggie...I know the song says everyone needs a bosom for a pillow, but I don't think this is what they meant" she was being suffocated in the matronly cuddle. Aggie released her and rummaged in her handbag for a tissue.

"Oh, dear I've started early..." she was blubbing as Peggy patted her shoulder in a comforting manner. The moment was broken as Seb, Rachel and Mhairi arrived at their side.

"Why's mum crying?" Seb asked Gavin, when he didn't get a response, he looked over to find Gavin blubbing too. "Oh, for god's sake what's happened to you all?" He looked at them as if they had all gone mad.

"Never mind Seb, I'll explain it later. We better take our seats ladies, or we will be run over by the brides." Rachel said calmly as she took Aggie and Peggy and led them to their seats and Mhairi shoved a still crying Gavin towards the front of the aisle to stand. She rolled her eyes as Bill came up to the group.

"He's always the same at weddings" explained Mhairi as Seb walked back towards the door and led Kate through. Ellie's heart stopped; Kate had never looked so beautiful. Her dress fitted her like a glove and her hair was pinned to her head in an elegant bun with a few face-framing pieces of hair cascading down. She held her bouquet of flowers in one hand and in the other was a silver topped cane. Ellie was lost for words; all she did was stare at her bride in awe. Kate giggled a little, she hadn't expected this reaction but was pleased, nonetheless. It was all she could do to keep calm herself as Ellie's long dark hair was plaited and falling over her shoulder. Kate thought she looked like an ancient high priestess with her dark features and high cheekbones. The ivory suit trousers hung low on her waist and the waistcoat fit her perfectly. Kate's pulse quickened when she met Ellie's eyes. This was it.

Bill took Ellie's arm and Seb took Kate's flower laden arm and they started up the aisle. Bill was marching as Ellie squeezed "Not too fast dad, nice and slow to make sure Kate doesn't stumble" she whispered. Bill slowed his pace, and everyone was safely delivered to the front of the room where the celebrant was standing. It was then that Ellie noticed him for the first time, he had a black eye, cauliflower ear and a neck brace on. He had the vacant gaze of someone who was punch drunk. Ellie looked at Kate who shrugged her shoulders. He spots them at last and a huge grin spread over what's left of his battered face.

"I need to explain…I was playing rugby yesterday and I got into a little bit of a tussle…but it's ok…I've got these lovely pain killers" he grinned as he rattled a bottle at them. He stood staring at them, they stared back…this wasn't going well. Ellie cleared her throat to focus him.

"Oh..yes yes of course. Hello everyone, my name is Stephen Simms, and I am the celebrant who will be…um…" he looked blank again and then stage whispered, "Why am I hear again?"

"A wedding" hissed Mhairi.

"Oh, am I getting married?" he cried happily "Who's the lucky lady?" he asked looking hopefully at both Kate and Ellie. "Oh no! I'm here to do the wedding aren't I?" he giggled and then shook his head as if to clear it, he had obviously forgot that the neck brace was there for a reason and he let out a yelp of pain.

"S'alright…I've got these pain killers" he said dreamily as he shook the pills at them once more.

"Oh, for the love of God come on you, shift yourself." muttered Peggy who had seen enough. She shooed him away to sit down, he waved 'bye-bye' to everyone as he was placed in a chair by Gavin. "Playing bloody rugby…good job I'm an ordained celebrant myself" she muttered.

"Peggy why are you ordained?" asked Kate.

"I had a protection job to do a few years ago and it seemed appropriate that I should be as close as possible to where the groom was standing." She said matter of factly. "Now let's get this show on the road" she turned towards Kate and Ellie.

"Now I know neither of the two of you wanted any faff so I'll make this to the point and then we can get on with the party" there were chuckles all round, except Aggie who had obviously been looking forward to some pomp and circumstance.

"Ok Eleanor McVey do you pledge to share your life openly with Katherine Mitchell, to be on this journey together and share your dreams as you go forward together and be her companion along the way?" Peggy asked.

"I do" Ellie said simply and smiled at Kate.

"Good start, Kate you next. Katherine Mitchell, do you pledge to share your life openly with Eleanor McVey, to be on this journey together and share your dreams as you go forward together and be her companion along the way?"

"I do" Kate said.

"Good, good, we're flying now." said Peggy "Now we need to do the legal bit, who has the rings?" she asked as Gavin stepped forward and handed Ellie a ring.

"Ellie repeat after me, I Eleanor McVey take you Katherine Mitchell to be my wife under law. I make this pledge freely, with honesty and sincerity and with a commitment that will grow deeper as the years pass. I give you this ring as a token of my love and a sign of the promises I make to you today"

Ellie repeated the vow, her eyes never leaving Kate's, as she placed the simple gold band on her finger.

"And now Kate" Peggy said, although she was starting to tear up. Rachel handed a ring to Kate and took her flowers off her.

"I Katherine Mitchell take you Eleanor McVey to be my wife under law. I make this pledge freely, with honesty and sincerity and with a commitment that will grow deeper as the years pass. I give you this ring as a token of my love and a sign of the promises I make to you today" Kate said with a shaking voice, as she placed the ring on Ellies finger, Kate's nerves had got the better of her and the moment threatened to overwhelm her. She could barely look at Ellie as she made her vow, fearing it would be too much for her. Her legs were wobbling already.

"Well, I think that covers everything" Peggy said lightly "So it gives me the greatest pleasure of my life to say that I now pronounce you married. Welcome to the family Ellie, you may kiss." she said with a smile as cheers erupted from the seated guests. Ellie grinned as she sealed her promise with a kiss. She whispered in Kate's ear "I can't believe you didn't look at me" she said it in jest knowing that Kate had a problem being centre of attention and panicked about public speaking more than anyone would ever know, the technique of not using eye contact helped.

"Shut up I'm mortified, I thought I was going to collapse. Sorry honey" she replied sheepishly but Ellie just laughed and squeezed her hand. "Look on the bright side, this is the last time we ever need to do this"

"Oh, that's right...we never have to plan or attend our wedding stuff ever again." Kate was elated at the prospect of getting her weekend mornings back.

"Ok you two, you nee to sign the register with your witnesses. Ann and Aggie could you step forward please? Everyone else if you could please make your way into the next room where refreshments have been laid on for you." There was a screeching of chairs as people started to file out in search of drinks. Kate and Ellie signed the wedding certificate, followed by Ann and Aggie as their witnesses and finally Peggy signed as celebrant.

"I better get him sent home in a taxi" pegged nodded in the direction of Stephen who was gaping at the colours of the stained-glass window like it was a kaleidoscope, pure joy on his face.

"Before you do, get the name of those pain killers for me" muttered Aggie.

Chapter 34

A small reception party was planned in the same room that the wedding took place, so in order for the staff to get the room ready, everyone was in the smaller bar area having drinks and eating the snacks placed on tables around the room. Night-time guests had started to arrive, once Kate and Ellie walked through to the room they were greeted by young Mark, Ellie's informant who had brought his formidable mother with him.

"Alright Ellie how ye doin? Thanks, and all that for asking us to come to the do. Here, we got you a little something. I promise I didn't nick it" he added hastily as he handed over a beautifully wrapped gift box.

"Thanks Mark, I'm glad you could make it, I must say you look downright handsome in your suit" Ellie said with a smile, his mum was already making her way towards the bar after a smile and a handshake to Ellie…she never was one for many words.

"Mark, you look very dapper" Kate said brightly as she leaned up to kiss his cheek. Mark turned scarlet but he was pleased at the compliments.

"I better go see what my maw is up to, she promised the doctor that she would cut down on the beer, so I better make sure she does. I want a dance with each of you later though." he grinned as he disappeared into the throng near the bar.

As Ellie's team arrived, Kate excused herself to go speak to Martha and her publisher and the woman they had brought with them.

"Hiya boss, great party" beamed Harris as Kent handed over the gift that the team had clubbed together to get.

"Thank you all for coming, I must say you all scrub up well" quipped Ellie as it was clear her team had made an effort, beautiful dresses and kilt suits were worn by all.

"Has there been any progress in the case?" she asked but before they could answer, a large hand clamped itself over Ellie's mouth from behind.

"I order you not to answer her, Els for Christ's sake it's your wedding, switch off!" joked Gavin as Ellie wrestled herself free from his grasp. She slapped his arm and then he slapped her back. Kent and Harris looked on awkwardly as their DI and their Detective Superintendent started a slapping match like a pair of children.

"Gavin Bickerton what do you think you are doing?!" Peggy roared as Gavin had succeeded in getting Ellie into a headlock. She grabbed him by the ear and marched him off towards where his Aunt Janet had just arrived. Peggy, still holding onto Gavin's ear, spoke briefly to Janet before handing Gavin over. Janet promptly slapped him in the back of the head.

“Ok you two…tell me the progress…that’s an order” Ellie added, attempting to regain her authority as if she hadn’t been fighting like an 8-year-old. Kent looked at Harris and then rolled her eyes.

“Fine, but I’ll be quick, the young soldier that died of the overdose? We don’t have too much on him yet, but we know that his name was Toby, still waiting on a surname, and that he came from a military family. Apparently, they pushed for an internal enquiry for years after.”

“Military family? Anyone still serving?” Ellie asked, he mind kicking into gear.

“No, he was the youngest of three, his older brother and sister were apparently in the forces too, we are still chasing their details.” Kent said.

“We’ve also tracked down the taxi driver that took Val home after your rehearsal.” Harris continued. “He confirms her timing, but it doesn’t clear her though.”

“Indeed, it doesn’t” muttered Ellie as she spotted Val across the room. Val was glaring at Seb and Rachel sharing a tender kiss. She then watched Val moved towards Kate, she whispered something in her ear and Kate said something back that Ellie could not hear before she turned her back and walked away.

“Ma’am, your wife is heading this way, we best not discuss the case” Kent said tactfully as Kate arrived at Ellie’s side. She looked a little angry, there was a flush creeping up her neck. Ellie’s team melted away into the crowds as Ellie turned Kate towards her.

“You ok sweetie? I saw Val having words with you” Ellie

asked gently.

"It's nothing, she's just angry." Kate said in clipped tones, she realised she was being a little short with Ellie and sighed. "I went to see her last night...after mum told us that story...it made my blood boil. It explained so much as to why we never saw them...I always thought it was after she slapped me. Anyway, I decided that I didn't want anything from her, it would be tainted now. So, I went to her house to return the Sapphire necklace."

"What Sapphire necklace asked Peggy from behind her"

"The one she said she was passing on; it was her grandmothers she said. It was clear she didn't want to give it to me and after last night, I didn't want it. So, I gave it back. She was livid...still is...said I'm no longer part of her family." Kate said shrugging.

"Her loss Katie." Peggy said as she placed an arm around her niece, but Ellie could have sworn she saw a triumphant twinkle in Peggy's eye, almost as if the information she had just found out was solid gold.

Chapter 35

The wedding party were called outside to take the wedding photos. The Old Church that Oran Mor had once been, was a beautiful backdrop to the photos. The photographer was set up and waiting.
"Ah good, first of all can I have the brides please." Instructed the photographer, who was a young man with trousers too short and no socks which set Aggie's teeth on edge, but Peggy whispered that it was a boho style as she nudged her. Ellie and Kate stood together, smiling at each other for a perfect pose in front of the stained-glass windows.

"Lovely ladies, thank you. Now can I get one with you and the parents please?" Kate and Ellie grabbed Peggy and Ann's hands to include them with Bill and Aggie. "You both have been second mothers to both of us, your place is here" Kate said as they all posed for further pictures. Ellie and Gavin as best man were next, followed by Kate with Mhairi and Rachel as bridesmaids.

"Excellent, could we finally have a group picture of the entire bridal party?" As the photographer set up for the shot, everyone gathered around Kate and Ellie. Before they could take the picture though, Val stumbled out of the entrance, spilling the drink in her hand. She had a nasty sneer on her face as she took in the view before her.

"Well, isn't this nice…all the family together, eh? Except it's not all the family, is it? It's all *your* family Agnes. You'd think Katherine never had a father, why wasn't I included eh? I mean you'll have some freaks in your pictures but not your own auntie?" she screeched malevolently as she pointed towards Seb and Rachel. That did it, Aggie walked straight up to the drunk and swaying Val and punched her squarely in the jaw, knocking her out cold. "Ouch" she winced as she wrung her hand "That was bloody sore, this is why I don't hit people" she said as she returned to her position in the group as if nothing had happened. The photographer wasn't sure what to do as Val was technically in the shot. He was about to move his camera tripod, but Peggy stopped him.

"Young man if you attempt to move that old crone out of shot you will join her on the pavement. Please ensure you take the picture exactly as it is. I'm sure everyone here would agree that they want this moment immortalised. The group as one said, "Oh yeah!" The photographer shrugged and took and the picture. The final official wedding photo showed the wedding party either laughing or with beaming smiles, completely ambivalent to the plight of the unconscious woman who lay at their feet.

"She wanted in the picture…now she is" Aggie said with satisfaction.

Chapter 36

In the function room the Master of Ceremonies called everyone to order. "Ladies and Gentlemen, will you please be upstanding for the Mrs McVey-Mitchells!" Cheers and wolf whistles rang out and Ellie and Kate walked in hand in hand to take their place at the head table. Once they were seated, he continued. "The bridal party aren't fans of wedding meals or formal speeches or any of the other faff involved in a wedding – their words ladies and gentlemen. So, they have arranged a buffet meal for everyone to help themselves whenever they feel hungry, the bar is stocked and the disco will commence soon, enjoy the evening everyone." More cheers followed this as people got up to either line up for the buffet or the bar. Bill, in an instant of chivalry, had shouted everyone down and had got plates of pakora, burgers, fries and pizza for the ladies at the main table. Gavin disappeared and returned with two mountainous plates of food, one for him and one for Mhairi who looked hungry enough to eat the weaker members of the party. Although there were to be no speeches, Bill got up when most of the room had re-seated themselves.

"Folks, I'm not going to take up too much of your time. I just want to say that this is a proud day for me and for the rest of the family up here. I want you to all charge your glasses and be upstanding...To Ellie and Kate" he called as he raised his pint of beer upwards.

"To Ellie and Kate" called the room, more wolf whistles, and cheers.

The food and drink flowed as people enjoyed the buffet and came up to congratulate the couple with a round of drinks. As Ellie and Kate didn't drink, they kept passing them off to Gavin, Ann, Bill, Peggy, and Aggie who were getting more and more drunk as the evening went on.

The Master of Ceremonies was back.

"Ladies and Gentlemen please gather round as the happy couple take to the floor for their first dance."

Ellie took Kate's hand and slowly led her to the dancefloor. The first chords of 'Truly Madly Deeply' started to play as Ellie took the lead and started a slow swaying movement in the middle of the dancefloor.

"Tell me if your leg can't take this" she said quietly into Kate's ear as they swayed together gently to the music.

"I'm fine honestly honey...this is perfect" Kate said as she nuzzled into Ellie's neck. There were 'awww' noises from the audience surrounding them and applause whenever they attempted a fancy turn when they got more confident. After a while Bill led Aggie on to the dancefloor, Seb & Rachel next, Gavin got up with Ann and, to the surprise of everyone, young Mask escorted Peggy to the floor and started a rather complicated waltz with her. Mhairi was sitting down, rubbing her stomach, and enjoying watching the others dance.

Ellie and Kate were in their own world for the duration of the song, they traded soft kisses and loving words as they swayed together. They only stopped when the song ended, and the DJ changed to a more up-tempo number to get the floor filled. They walked back to their seats to drink and watch their closest friends and family enjoy themselves. They remained there until the first few notes of 'Beautiful Sunday' started to play.

"Oh my god it's the Slosh!" screamed Mhairi as she struggled to her feet. Ellie was about to turn to Kate when she noticed she was gone. Kate was off like a dog out of the traps towards the dancefloor. In fact, Ellie was the only woman left in her seat within ten seconds, Aggie, Peggy, Ann, Mhairi, Rachel, Kate, Gavin's Aunt Janet and even Mark's mum were all doing the moves in time to the music. Bill took the seat vacated by Kate and shook his head as he watched the spectacle.

"Why have they all gone mad?" he asked his daughter in confusion.

"The Slosh dad…it's like catnip to Scottish women. I've never met one that could resist it" she explained with amusement as she watched them all dance away.

As the night wore on drinks flowed and inhibitions went out the window. Bill and Peggy were dancing together like they were stuck to each other in the slow numbers. Mark had cornered Kent at the bar and was trying all his moves to make her laugh…and he was succeeding! Gavin and Seb had their ties round their heads and were doing an air guitar stand off with each other, which was impressive as the song being played was 'C'est La Vie' by B*Witched.

Ellie decided the time was right to go when Run Rig's version of 'Loch Lomond' started to play and a group of drunken Scottish people huddled in the middle of the dancefloor to sing along with the words. She took Kate's hand and led her towards the exit, only Peggy saw them leave, she waived across to them before continuing to sing in the middle of the crowd.

When they walked outside, they realised that it had started to snow while they were inside. Byres Road was oddly silent as the snow muffled their footsteps as they walked across the road to the hotel in which they planned to spend their wedding night in each other's arms.

Chapter 37

The morning sun was bright as it shone through the windows of the honeymoon suite. Ellie was wrapped around Kate who was still in a deep sleep, the fingers that now held their wedding rings were entwined together. They had got little sleep as their long night together had been too perfect to let it end. Ellie kissed Kate's shoulder as she gently got out of bed to order room service coffee and croissants for breakfast. Kate stirred as Ellie returned to the bed.
"Mmmm morning sweetie." She murmured happily as she turned to face Ellie. They kissed gently and smiled at each other. "Morning" whispered Ellie. "How do you feel this morning?" she asked.

"I'll let you know when the rest of me wakes up" quipped Kate as she stretched and stifled a yawn. "Although I'm kind of regretting the fact that we aren't getting ready to jet off on honeymoon" she confessed. They had decided to postpone the honeymoon until the summer as they were so busy. If they had gone now, all the relaxation would have been for nothing as they would come home to very hectic schedules.

"How bad do you think it got after we left?" Ellie asked as Kate grabbed her phone.

"God knows with that lot, nothing on Facebook yet so I imagine no one is awake yet. Oh, but there's a message from mum, she's got all the presents sent over to ours so we've not to worry about them".

There was a knock at the door and Ellie pulled on a robe as she made her way to the door. The porter struggled in with the breakfast trolley, he was hobbling on a crutch.

"I'm sorry about this, we're short staffed today and I'm still on the mend from a car accident." he explained in apology as Ellie helped him in with the breakfast. Ellie stopped in her tracks as her eyes fixed on the crutch, she missed what he was saying to her. Kate knew that look in her eyes, but the Porter was looking at her like he had done something wrong.

"Thank you for bringing this up, I hope your leg gets better soon" Kate said from the bed. He smiled and hobbled back out. Ellie snapped out of her reverie and brought the tray to the bed, still deep in thought.

"What's wrong honey?" Kate asked.

"Dunno…something about that guy's crutch has kicked something in my brain…but I'm too tired to make sense out of it." her brain was being sluggish, and she wished the fog would clear.

"Is it work related?" Kate asked as Ellie handed her a coffee and a chocolate croissant.

"Probably" she admitted as she tried to switch off and enjoy their time together. They settle down to their breakfast and enjoy a happy half hour talking and kissing.

"What have we got to do today?" asked Ellie as she cleared their plates away.

"Well...Martha wants to meet me this afternoon, she needs to run through some things with me...would you mind?" Kate asked quietly.

"No, not at all. This is why we postponed the honeymoon; busy schedules remember. Whatever you need to do honey, is fine with me, besides I'm sure someone will need to round up our guests from wherever they ended up last night." Ellie joked as Kate got out of bed. All that dancing had taken its toll on her, she was limping very badly, and she needed to grab the cane from the side of the bed in order to make it to the bathroom. This image triggered what it was that Ellie's brain had been trying to tell her. She gasped as she sat bolt upright in the bed. "I know who the murderer is!"

Chapter 38

Ellie and Kate were driving home, Ellie had spent the past hour making calls to her team as Kate showered and got dressed. A plan was in motion that Ellie hoped would sort this case out once and for all. They got home to find carnage before them. Peggy was making a huge fry-up wearing a nightie and Garfield slippers. Aggie and Ann were passed out on the couches in the outfits they were wearing yesterday, Ann was cuddling a shoe like a teddy bear and Bill was sat at the table with an Alka seltzer fizzing in a glass in front of him, his head in his hands.

"Did we all have fun then?" Kate bellowed from the door as they assembled hungover party groaned.

"Have mercy, we're too old to be drinking like this." cried Ann from her prone position.

"How's your hand today mum?" Kate asked Aggie who had a sizeable bruise on her knuckles.

"Bloody sore, that Val always was hard-headed." She complained.

"Anyone know what happened to her?" Ellie asked.

"She wasn't there after the first dance; I was out for a smoke, and she was gone" explained Ann.

"I should go over and apologise to her." muttered Aggie.

"Will you hell!" shouted Peggy from the kitchen. "Think of it as payback, she was being horrible, and she deserved it…in fact she deserved it long before yesterday."

"Still…I should probably check on her." Aggie said guiltily.

"No need Aggie, I'm heading that way today, so I'll check she's still alive." offered Ellie.

"And if she isn't, let me know so I can plan the party." shouted Peggy. "Do you girls want any breakfast?"

"No thanks Peggy, I've got to go meet Gavin." Ellie answered.

"Nonsense, here take a roll and bacon with you, I've made it just the way you like it. Here's one for my boy too." Peggy said as she handed over two wrapped breakfast rolls. Gavin was now 'her boy'.

"Be careful" Kate said quietly as Ellie walked towards the door. Ellie had explained her plan on the journey home.

"I promise I will, I'll call you later honey." She gave Kate a quick kiss and left the house to the sound of groaning as Peggy set large plates of greasy food in front of everyone.

Chapter 39

Ellie pulled up outside Gavin's house and waited for his appearance, she took a large bite of the bacon roll that Peggy had made her and groaned in delight, she hadn't realised how hungry she was. A fragile and broken looking Gavin walked gingerly towards her. When he got in the car, he looked miserable.
"What's up buttercup?" Ellie asked breezily as she tossed him a roll which he devoured with indecent happiness.

"I'm getting too old for the dashing white sergeant" he muttered around mouthfuls of bacon. "Aunt Janet was birling me about like she was working the waltzers, she's done something to my back"

"Poor baby" Ellie crooned as he elbowed at her.

"Anyway, back to murder and mayhem, have we got a location?" Ellie asked as she crumpled up the paper her roll was in.

"Aye Kent has eyes on at the Community Centre, she's holding for us." Gavin explained as he fished painkillers out of his pocket and washed them down with a bottle of water that he found in the back of Ellie's car.

"Excellent, how's Mhairi today? She still sore?" Ellie asked as they moved through traffic towards the community centre.

"Not really, she didn't have a great night but she's finally sleeping now. Janet has stayed with her; she's getting one of her cronies to open the bar for her. She says if Mhairi is still in pain when she wakes up, she'll get the doctor out to her.

"Good, I'm glad she's got someone with her. If you need to go home today, just do it, can't be too careful" Ellie said as they finally pulled in behind Kent outside the Community Centre.

"Thanks Els…hopefully there will be no need, eh?" he said quietly.

Kent had got out of her car and trotted over to get into the back of Ellie's.

"Morning ma'am, there's been no movement since they all went in about half an hour ago." she explained as she leaned forward between the front seats.

"Good, did you bring those files I asked for?" Ellie asked as Kent seemed ready for the question and handed over some files. "Good work Kent" she said as she scanned the information in the top file. She found the information that confirmed her suspicions.

"How do you want to do this Els?" asked Gavin as he took the file from her and scanned it himself.

"Softly softly I think, we'll go in and confront them with what we know…see if they confess. If not, then we have enough suspicion for a warrant to search the house. We ready?" she asked as she got out of the car and headed towards the Community Centre.

Inside the support group was in full swing, the chatter stopped when they walked in though. All eyes turned towards them, but Ellie was looking past them towards the tea station where Val looked pale around her bruised eyes.

"You know why we're here; do you want to come quietly? It will be easier on you." Ellie said loudly. All eyes spun to the back of the room to await a response.

"Aye it's ok hen...I'll come quietly" Doreen said as she picked up her stick and walked slowly towards them. Val collapsed into a chair clutching her chest

Chapter 40

Ellie and Gavin walk into the interview room where Doreen calmly sat waiting for them. Gavin placed a tape into the machine and stated who was in the room as well as the time and date. Once this was done, Ellie started the interview.

"Doreen, can you confirm that you have refused council to be with you during this interview?"

"Yes, I don't need a lawyer at this time." She said quietly but still calmly as she toyed with a cup of coffee.

"Doreen, I understand you served in the Military Police, what regiment were you attached to?" Ellie started.

"I was an NCO with the Military Provost Staff Corps for over 30 years. I spent most of my service stationed at Queen's Barracks in Perth with the Royal Regiment of Scotland." Doreen answered with pride.

"You are from a military family?"

"Yes...my father served during the war and both my brothers joined up when they were old enough."

"Yes, I noticed that in your file...do you want to talk about your brother Toby?" Ellie asked gently. Doreen smiled sadly as she took herself back in her memory.

"Toby was always a sweet boy, devoted to me when he was young. When he was going through basic training, he was in a barracks not far from me and I tried to keep an eye on him. He loved being in the army...one of the boys and all that." She chuckled.

"It wasn't until he joined the 6th battalion that his trouble started. He was easy led you see, even as a kid if someone said to do something daft, he would...drove our mum daft that did. I got word through from an MP at his barracks that he was behaving in a strange way...he worried that drugs might be the reason as there had been a huge uptake in drug use there at the time. I tried to talk to Toby about it, but he shut me out, in the end he ignored my calls completely. Then I got the call...he had died from a suspected overdose. I had to go identify him...couldn't let my mum go through that and my other brother Alan was overseas at the time."

"I'm sorry about your brother...did you find out who gave him the drugs?" Ellie pushed. Doreen looked her straight in the eye before she answered.

"You know I did...it was Eric. We tried through every official channel over the years to get an enquiry through... but it was all hushed up and Eric redeployed. It was only this past year that I realised by luck that I had retired to a street that Eric was living in...then I knew it was fate."

“You tried to kill him” Ellie said as a fact rather than a question.

“Yes…and without sounding like a scooby doo villain, I would have killed him if not for Val catching up to me and interrupting, I had to move quickly around so that she didn’t know I had been there with Eric.”

“Why then, did you kill Kai and Mick later that night?”

“I’ve volunteered at that support group almost since I moved here, I’ve heard all their stories and the pain caused…I felt it was my moral duty to rid each of the families of the person who caused them the pain. I thought that it would put right what happened with Toby somehow…so when Val fell asleep, I looked out and couldn’t believe my luck that I spotted him outside. I left Val’s quietly and followed him…I hit him from behind before he knew anyone was there…he had those headphone things in you see.”

“You hit him with your crutch?”

“Yes, when can I have that back?” Doreen asked.

“We are conducting forensic tests on it at the moment.”

“But there’s no need…you’ll find some…I’m admitting it”

“I know, but we still have to. So, you killed Kai and then how did you meet Mick?” Ellie continued.

“I was walking back to Val’s; I took a route that I knew I wouldn’t need to walk past Bobby’s house as he really is a nosey beggar at times, and I thought it best he didn’t see me out and about. I was heading towards the chemist when I saw that one Michael, it’s like it was meant to be, two of them out alone one the same night!” Doreen said with energy.

“You followed him?” Ellie pushed.

“I did, he was relieving himself behind the bins…mucky brute. I waited for a moment and then I hit him too. I left him where he was, I couldn’t move him if I tried. After that I walked back to Val’s as fast as I could.”

“So you got to Val’s without any further incident?”

“Yes, I just got sat down when she started to stir…I figured if I woke her, then I had an alibi, so I woke her and sent her to bed and I left.”

“You admit to killing Kai and Mick…what about the other men?”

“Yes, I killed them too, that last one managed to get a punch in to my leg. I had a list you see…you’ll find it in my bedside cabinet when you search my house. I had planned to get every name on the list and then, if I hadn’t been caught, I would turn myself in as a matter of honour. It’s a shame I didn’t get all of them…the world would be a cleaner place.” She said matter of factly.

Ellie had heard enough. She formally charged Doreen with several counts of murder and one count of attempted murder.

“I understand…what will happen to me now?”

“You will be held on remand until a trial date can be fixed…I advise you get counsel though; they may be able to fix you up with bail until then.” Ellie explained.

“Thanks…you’re a good lassie.” Doreen said quietly before returning her attention to her coffee as Ellie left the room.

Chapter 41

In the office Ellie and the team are winding down with beers and soft drinks. She stands up to whistles and cheers.

"I just wanted to thank each and every one of you for the work you've done on this case, especially given the time frame...we've cleared more unsolved murders in one case than other teams clear up in a year so give yourselves a pat on the back and I've called the Royal Oak and put money behind the bar for all of you to go and celebrate tonight so get yourselves out of here for the day." This was met with cheers as they all departed leaving just Ellie and Gavin.

"You not going with them?" Ellie asked as she looked at an email from forensics. "Preliminary tests show several different DNA traces on Doreen's crutch, so it looks like we have the evidence to go with her confession" she said as she read.

“Nah I don’t fancy the pub tonight...I’m probably just going to shoot off home, see how Mhairi is if that’s ok?”

“Yeah of course, in fact if you give me five minutes to finish this report, I’ll drop you off.” Just then, Ellie’s phone rang, it was Kate.

“Hi honey, I’ll be home soon...” Ellie began but Kate talked over her.

“Never mind that, is Gavin with you?!” Kate demanded urgently.

“Well...yes why what’s wrong?”

“Why is his phone off?! Janet’s been ringing him for an hour!”

“Oh shit, Gav your phone is still off. Sorry honey we turn them off when interviewing...what’s wrong?”

“Mhairi’s went into labour that’s what’s wrong! She’s up to high doe as she couldn’t get hold of him so get him over to the Queen Elizabeth now!” Kate bellowed as she hung up. Ellie didn’t need to relay the instructions; she had been loud enough for Gavin to hear, and he went into panic mode.

“Where’s my car keys?! Ellie where the hell are my keys?!” he shouted as he tossed things off his desk.

“I don’t know, I’ll help you look.” she ran over to the desk and started emptying the drawers before coming to her senses.

“Oh, for Christ’s sake you don’t have your keys, I drove you!” she rolled her eyes at her own stupidity before she grabbed her keys and ran after Gavin towards the car park.

Technically she wasn't supposed to use the blue lights for anything other than official police business, but this was an emergency Ellie decided as they gunned her car towards the Clyde tunnel and to the hospital. Miraculously they found a parking space just about to be vacated close to the entrance. Ellie waited patiently for the elderly man to start to manoeuvre his car out of the space which was proving difficult due to how close the next car was to him. Gavin had no such patience right now.

"Oh, for god's sake if you want something doing..." he muttered as he got out of the car and ran towards the other driver. Ellie watched as Gavin got the old man out and then proceeded to back the car out himself before getting out and getting an earful from the man. Ellie chose not to intervene as she pulled into the space. When she got out the man was finishing his diatribe. "...young folk have no patience...no respect..." but the rest fell on deaf ears as both Gavin and Ellie tore off in the direction of maternity.

When they burst into the waiting room they were met by Kate, Janet, and Peggy. Gavin said one breathless word "where?" Janet pointed to the door opposite, and he ran off to find Mhairi. Ellie sat down beside Kate to wait.

"Sorry I shouted down the phone at you" Kate said with an apologetic kiss. "Mhairi was beside herself that she couldn't get Gavin. Peggy and I were visiting to see how she was and then all hell broke loose"

"Don't apologise, it was a stressful situation, Gavin just forced an old man out of his car because he wasn't reversing quickly enough so it's a stressful kind of day" Ellie said with a smile as she laced their fingers together and tried to relax after the mad dash.

"Did you get her?" Kate said quietly.

"We did, she confessed to it all and there's DNA on her crutch...sad really... saw Val at the centre too. She's got two black eyes but otherwise alive...although when she saw me, she went white as a sheet." Ellie said with confusion.

"Ah...that might have something to do with the fact that she also had a visit from the police this morning." Peggy said with a knowing smile.

"What?" Kate asked as she sat up quickly. "Why?"

"Something to do with family history" Peggy said evasively as she inspected her nails.

"Peggy...what did you do?!" Kate almost shrieked but was calmed by Ellie's hand on her arm.

"I'll tell you a wee tale about your family history...how about that?" Peggy offered. Ellie answered quickly before Kate could protest.

"Go ahead Peggy."

"Well as you know Katie, your great grandmother Beryl gave Val that necklace as a family heirloom and then she passed it to you?" Kate nodded and Peggy continued.

"Well Val was under the impression that this had been handed down to her gran, from a great-great gran...but someone has done some digging in the family tree... traced these female relatives...and no one on there could possibly have been able to afford that necklace. They were all either crofters' wives from the islands or working-class folk from the inner-city slums of Victorian Glasgow."

“Right…so where did the necklace come from then?” Kate asked, her confusion calming her tone.

“Well, you see your Beryl worked as a housekeeper for some very prominent families back in the day. One in particular, was an American Army General stationed in Glasgow during the war. Now this General had married a local woman when he was stationed here, and they set up home in one of the grand mansions on Great Western Road at the time. Beryl worked in their home for about three months before she moved on to work in a munitions factory to help the war effort. It wasn’t until after the war, when they were packing to moves stateside, that the General’s wife realised that she was missing some items…jewellery mainly. Her husband contacted the police but as they could not ascertain when the theft took place, they were unable to find the thief or the jewellery. The General left for home without it. I think you can guess one of the particular items that was stolen?” Peggy asked.

“The necklace?” Kate whispered as Peggy nodded.

“In fact, when you look deeper into the time, there were quite a few thefts of this nature spanning from 1938-1944, all from large wealthy houses and none of the stuff was ever recovered. Beryl worked for every one of the victims at one point.” Peggy said quietly.

“So, granny Beryl was a jewel thief?” Kate said and then burst out laughing. “That’s brilliant, I mean it’s terrible but the fact she was never caught. That’s amazing” Kate continued to chuckle.

“So, you can imagine Val’s surprise when the police came to her door this morning along with a representative of the insurance company who had to pay out on the necklace all those years ago. They have now retrieved the necklace I'm led to believe and are looking through Val's house for any more of the loot." Peggy now couldn't contain her self-satisfied smirk as everyone started to chuckle at the image of Val having the police at her door.

"You're a crafty old bugger Peggy" Janet said, impressed as she wiped a tear from her eye as she continued to chuckle to herself.

"I told you I would get her. I just needed the angle." Peggy said as she settled back in her chair once more. That necklace was it; I knew that Val's family could never have been from money so I started doing a little digging...couldn't believe it when I found those police reports, it was like Christmas."

"Well, here's to Great-Granny Beryl, jewel thief extraordinaire." Kate said as she raised a cup of coffee in salute.

Their laughter was interrupted by Gavin coming back through the door looking like he had been hit with a bat. He was dazed but had the biggest smile on his face as he turned towards them all.

"I've got a boy and a girl!!" he bellowed as everyone rushed to hug and congratulate him.

"One of each eh, good on you. How's Mhairi?" Janet said matter of factly but her eyes were watering with pride.

"She's fine, sore and tired obviously but she's over the moon. Twenty fingers and twenty toes accounted for; they look like old men but I'm hoping they grow out of that" he quipped still grinning.

"Have you thought of names yet?" Kate said as she detangled herself from a bear hug.

"Oh yeah...um we're naming the boy Shaun, after Mhairi's brother and um...the girl...we're naming her Eleanor." He looked quickly at Ellie to gage a reaction, but Ellie grabbed him and gave him a huge hug. "I'm honoured" she whispered into his neck as everyone else cheered the names of the newest members of the family.

Epilogue

Two months had gone by since that day in the hospital. Spring was starting to creep slowly closer as daffodils were sprouting in the garden. Bill and Ann had come over on the ferry for a quick visit before they travelled on to Blackpool for some reunion weekend of old school friends.

"Why Blackpool though dad?" Ellie asked in confusion as she laid the table for dinner.

"We had a school trip there once; it was a hell of a trip and everyone there remembers it fondly so we thought we could recreate it." Bill said with a shrug.

"Aye and because of his year going on that trip, whatever they got up to ensured that it never happened again so my and my mates never got to go!" said Ann from the sofa where she sat drinking wine with Aggie and Mhairi as Gavin was changing two sets of nappies. He got up and placed both babies into a travel cot and walked into the kitchen looking tired but happy.

“Fatherhood suits you” joked Bill as he handed Gavin a beer.

“They are a handful already, but I wouldn’t be without them…except when Eleanor has a hissy fit and screams the place down when I put pink on her” he complained as Ellie chuckled.

“That’s my girl” she said with pride.

Gavin and Ellie had been at court all week as, although Doreen had pleaded guilty to all charges, they still needed to be present for victim statements before judgement. Doreen got sentenced to four life sentences and was taken to Corton Vale prison.

Peggy came in at that moment bursting with gossip.

“I’ve just seen Val! Oh, you should have seen her face.”

“Was it her court date already?” Aggie asked her sister.

“Oh yes, she was found guilty and has been placed on a tag. She’s even made it into the Digger!” Peggy was gleeful, the Digger was a local magazine that told all the lurid tales form local court hearings. “I might get it framed” she said as she pulled the magazine out of her bag and held it reverently. Val hadn’t taken the intrusion into her house by the police all that well. When they tried to take the necklace and some pearl earrings, she lost her temper and punched a female PC and the man from the insurance company. Today was her court date for the assaults.

“She’ll love being on a tag, it makes her exactly the same as the supposed thugs she’s been complaining about for years” said Aggie, and she too had a smile on her face, finally free of the past and her abusive in-laws.

“Oh, love I forgot, with all the excitement at your wedding, we never gave you your wedding present!" Bill said excitedly as Ann, Aggie and Peggy got up to join him.

"Now we know you two are putting off your honeymoon…but we all got together and clubbed in for one gift. We've bought you a cruise around Scandinavia!"

"That's brilliant, thanks everyone, I've always wanted to visit up that way" Ellie said excitedly as she and Kate hugged each of them in turn.

"We know, and here's the best bit, Peggy has a contact and was able to get a group rate for next to nothing so all of us are going on the cruise too!" Bill said and this wasn't met with the same enthusiasm.

"You're all going on our honeymoon cruise?" Kate asked with a fixed smile on her face although Ellie could see the panic in her eyes.

"Oh, would you look at her, she's so happy she's crying said Bill as he hugged his daughter-in-law.

"You've got plenty of time, the cruise isn't until August, but we couldn't wait to see your surprise."

Ellie could see Gavin and Mhairi having fits of laughter behind the four earnest faces in front of them. Seeing no way out of it without hurting their feelings she smiled "That's great, thank you so much, we can't wait to go, and we're glad you'll be joining us."

"Aye it's been too long since we've had a good old fashioned family holiday, and what better occasion than the joining of two families" Bill said, and Ellie smiled in earnest at the sweet nature of the gift.

Ann and Aggie broke out the brochure and was showing Kate all the facilities on board when Peggy turned to Ellie

"Oh Ellie love, there was an envelope sticking out of the letter box when I came in, it's addressed to you." She handed over the plain white envelope that had no address, just her name 'Ellie McVey'. As she opened it Gavin had wandered over and whispered in her ear "how are you going to get out of that family cruise eh?" he chuckled but it died in his throat as he looked down at the contents of the envelope. Ellie had gone pale, and Gavin sat her down as he grabbed his phone to make a call. Kate, worried, ran over to Ellie who was staring blindly down at what looked like a tarot card. She didn't understand why Ellie was in shock and Gavin looked terrified.

"Sir, I need you to find out exactly where John Peter Cotton is right now" Gavin said down the phone. "Prison? I think you might need to check that sir...Ellie got the death card sent to her house." Gavin hung up and looked Ellie in the eyes. "It's going to be ok Els, the Chief is sending armed officers to guard your house. It'll be ok Els, breathe..."

Ellie wasn't listening, her premonition years before was coming true. The bogeyman of her worst nightmares was back.

The End

Books By This Author

The Arc

Death On The Dream

Explosion In The Arts

Double Trouble

www.ingramcontent.com/pod-product-compliance
Ingram Content Group UK Ltd.
Pitfield, Milton Keynes, MK11 3LW, UK
UKHW021659190726
13853UKWH00001B/364